# SYMPHONY of *Grace*

## A Collection of Short Works

Edited by
**Anne Hamilton & Ruth Bonetti**

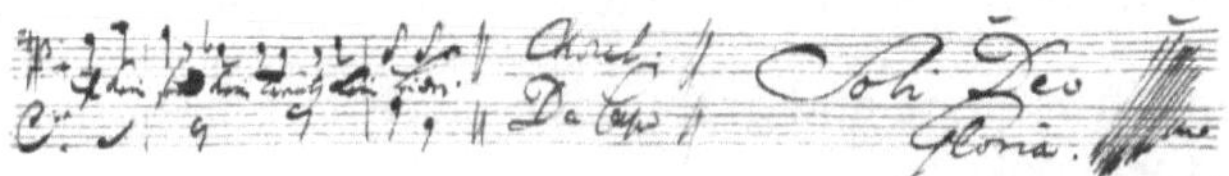


**Hazel Barker**

**Linda Barton**

**Antoni Bonetti** AM

**Ruth Bonetti**

**Diana Davison**

**Miranda de Jager**

**Rose Dee**

**M. Lester Dighton**

**Michelle Dennis Evans**

**Sandra Florentina**

**Terry Gatfield**

**Anne Hamilton**

**Dell Saddler Hamilton**

**Pamela Julian**

**Nola Lorraine**

**Rosemary New**

**Raelene Purtill**

**Rebekah Robinson**

**Karen Roper**

**Jo Wanmer**

**Jenny Woolsey**

**Justin Yeend**

*Symphony of Grace*

Anne Hamilton, Ruth Bonetti (editors)

© Individual contributors 2025

Published by Armour Books
P. O. Box 492, Corinda QLD 4075

Cover & interior design and typeset by Beckon Creative

Images: agsandrew, iStock | Material of Music stock photo;
J.S. Bach | Soli Deo Gloria

ISBN: 978-1-925380-83-5

 A catalogue record for this book is available from the National Library of Australia

All rights reserved. No part of this publication may be reproduced, stored in, or introduced into a retrieval system, or transmitted, in any form, or by any means (electronic, mechanical, photocopying, recording or otherwise) without the prior written permission of the publisher.

Note: Australian spelling and grammar conventions are used throughout this book.

Scripture citations

# SYMPHONY of Grace

## A Collection of Short Works

### Edited by
### Anne Hamilton & Ruth Bonetti

# Contents

## SECTION I – FICTION

## SECTION II – NONFICTION

## ABOUT THE AUTHORS     

# Introduction

## ANNE HAMILTON & RUTH BONETTI

'Again, truly I tell you that if two of you on earth agree about anything they ask for, it will be done for them by My Father in heaven.'

*Matthew 18:19* NIV

This volume of short stories and poems takes its title, *Symphony of Grace*, from the thought expressed in Jesus' remarkable promise about prayer. The word used in Matthew's gospel for *agree* means to be *in symphony, in accord, harmony* or *concord*.

The different voices of the twenty-two authors in this collection come together like the various instruments of an orchestra—some high and haunting, some bright and tinkling, some deep and profound. There's even a short story about an orchestra to round out this offering of praise to God in verse and prose.

Many authors would resonate with Johann Sebastian Bach, who frequently initialled his blank manuscript pages with the marking, 'J.J.' (*'Help me, Jesus'*) or I.N.J. (*'In the name of Jesus'*). At the manuscript end, Bach initialled the letters S.D.G. (*'Soli Deo Gloria'*, *'To God alone, the glory'*).

It's our prayer that these stories will resonate with you and fill your heart with hope, healing and wonder. May you be blessed beyond measure as you read.

Grace and peace,

*Anne + Ruth*

January 2025

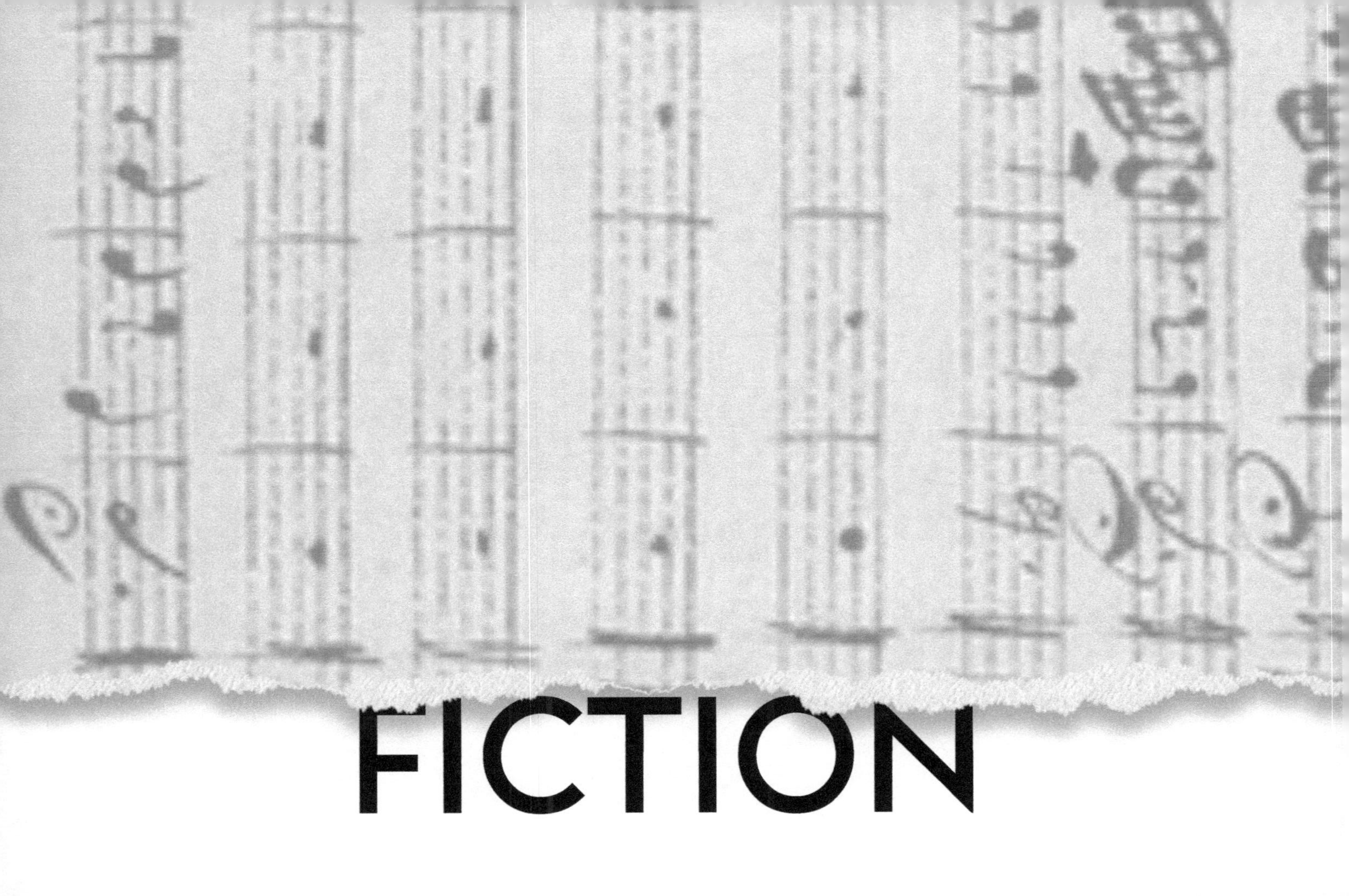
FICTION

# The Stoop

## REBEKAH ROBINSON

You think Him graceless. His words are harsh, you say; but I was there, I was the one on the receiving end, and I tell you—there is none more gracious than He. Let me share with you the full story.

We were desperate. My boy, he had a disability. He suffered from panolepsy. It caused pandemonium inside him. You think I use that word lightly. No, I don't. I mean it literally. *Pan. Demon. Ium.* His whole life he'd had seizures—not just the kind that make a person absent, or rigid, or trembling. We got the trifecta. My boy's seizures were like an arrest of his body and mind, sending both out of control. He flailed and screamed and gnashed his teeth. He foamed and shook violently. He threw himself into the fire or water, as if he wanted to end it all. It was terrifying. Only our love for him kept us from hightailing it out of there.

There were occasional moments of respite when my sweet boy emerged, broken and helpless, still unable to speak;

but on the whole, it was getting worse. Both body and soul were deteriorating horribly. And it broke our hearts. He was fourteen.

We took him to the Temple when he was little. They were quick to tell us that he was afflicted by an evil spirit. Well, *duh*. But they said there was nothing they could do. Casting out demons was the Messiah's forté, they said; and do you see a Messiah anywhere around here? 'No. Go home,' they said. 'Repent of everything you can think of. Come back and offer the appropriate sacrifices. And make a donation. Maybe God will intervene; but we've never seen it. Not even the great and prophetic King Saul could shed a demon.'

Well, that was about as helpful as a fishing net for a ceiling. We tried all that. Nothing. We attempted to be patient, but it just wasn't working.

So, we fished around for another approach. Clearly, this kind of panic—*pan-olepsy*—comes from Pan. The idea of getting involved with the hairy goat-god Pan—or Azazel the scapegoat, if you prefer the older identification—made the hairs on our arms stand up. But the demon was already involved with us. If sacrificing to the Lord wasn't going to help, maybe we could placate the driving spirit itself somehow. Hope it might let up a bit. Pay protection money, if you like. Any improvement would be way ahead of none.

The more we examined this idea, the more credence we gave it. Stupid, I know, but it's the place we were in. We didn't stop to think that maybe other consequences would follow. Like that it wouldn't be a one-time deal; like we'd have to keep on paying; like we'd have invited the thing into covenant with our family. And it would put paid to any covenant protection the Lord might still wish to give our household. I'd like to say I had no idea at the time what a big deal that really was... but that would be a lie. I went down this road on purpose. By the time we actually *met* the Lord, we were long gone.

We trekked all the way north to Panias, the place the Romans call Caesarea Philippi. It was rough going—days of walking over all kinds of terrain, struggling with my gangly son, whose demon tantrummed and taunted and rolled him away all the long way. I don't know if it saw what was coming, or it merely amped up the pressure to get us all more firmly into Azazel's clutches. It was hell just getting to the Gates of Hell.

Yeah, that's what they call it, the shrine of Pan at the base of Mount Hermon. There's an underground river, and huge gaping mouths, hungry for offerings and repellent acts. The people who hang around are fully pagan. By then, so were we. The theory was that if you did the right (very wrong) rituals, you could petition Hell for relief. Maybe.

None of that helped either. If Azazel was there, it was enjoying the whole thing; my son's exploitation did not ease one whit. We kept trying; it kept not working. Hell was laughing at us.

And then along came a really big band of people. Two of them stopped to talk to us, and it quickly became apparent they were followers of a rabbi named Yeshua. A rabbi with a difference: apparently he'd given them authority (what? how? unless he was the Messiah, haha?) to cast out demons and heal the sick.

So I shrugged and led them into the little house we'd rented, and showed them my son. They put their hands on his shoulders, and the demon writhed and made its usual inarticulate noises, only louder and more panicked than usual. They prayed. The demon shut up, all right, but it refused to leave, *and how!*

They seemed puzzled, like they'd actually expected a different result. They tried again. And just like everything else—it didn't work. They looked at each other, perplexed and a little afraid. So they mumbled their condolences and left, saying that Yeshua himself would be along presently. Whatever power they thought they'd had, it clearly wasn't as big as Azazel's. A new wave of hopelessness swamped me.

I really, really, really needed a *real* Messiah.

From Yahweh.

Nothing else was going to cut it. Yeah, pun about cutting covenant there, sorry about that.

I knew there was nothing in the Law or the Prophets that says the Messiah will be able to cast out demons. But some of the rabbis claim an old tradition that He'll even have the ability to expel deaf-and-dumb ones. The ones that the exorcists can't question to identify themselves by name and so get power over them. Besides, there's nothing that says He'll be able to magically multiply food, either, and I'd heard a really strange rumour out of Galilee about that, not long before. There was just the tiniest chance that the scribes were wrong, and there really *was* a Messiah at large.

What if this rabbi *can* help? Oh, but His delegates couldn't. That was my tortured thinking. What's the point in asking? *But what's the point in NOT asking?*

I went 'round and 'round this dilemma for the best part of a week, while my son thrashed and convulsed and moaned and ground his teeth down some more. I was done with Pan. The goat-demon wasn't interested in helping; Yeshua's disciples, for all their incompetence, had at least given it a go...

And then He arrived. Not from the road, but from the mountain.

My son had caused a scene. Again. A group gathered, as they do when there's a spectacle. The vultures! I explained what I was doing there. Nobody looked askance at me; they were all in Panias for the same thing, after all—spiritual intervention. Any kind, really.

So when four figures were seen trudging down the sacred mountain where the gods of the nations were said to live, the crowd rushed to see who they were. Why were their faces shining? Was it a trick of the light? Which one of them was the rabbi? Why would a rabbi be *here?*

He turned out to be the nondescript one the other three gave deference to, not the big surly one or the thunderous-looking pair, who would have been my first choices.

I shouted. He heard me. He listened. He got angry. I deserved it. He knew full well what it meant, me and my boy being at Panias, the *Pan-shrine*, in the first place. This was not a place where people sought Yahweh. I had some nerve to even approach Him. But I was all out of options, and ready to try God again, in the final extremity.

And Rabbi Yeshua? 'How long do I have to put up with this kind of unbelieving deviance?' he demanded. 'Pan? Seriously?' But then He lowered His voice and started asking more concerned questions. We both knew the Lord God had been putting up with spiritual perversity for a very, very long time, though not without warnings. For all His outburst, Yeshua didn't turn His back and leave, which surprised me. He had a little patience left in Him, and a lot of kindness, too. So maybe God did, too...

Then He was ready to see my boy.

Well, the demon did not like that one bit. It was only going to let go over my son's dead body. It threw him down with a full display of its horrible powers, as if to kill him right in front of Life.

And this told me one thing: whatever was in Yeshua was the opposite of what was in my son. It. Felt. *Threatened*. Finally!

Yeshua did not look worried. I couldn't be sure what He was feeling; there were fleeting expressions of sadness, indignation, but overriding all of that, in the end... compassion.

'Can You do anything?' I pleaded.

'*Can* I? All things are possible to him who believes!' Did He mean His own belief, or mine? Or both? *ALL* things? *Truly?* Was this... it?

I burst into tears. 'I do believe!' I wanted to. But He saw right through me. I switched to total honesty. 'Help my unbelief!' I wailed.

The crowd thickened. He wasted no more time.

He rebuked the spirit.

It reacted. Violently.

And... it left.

There was silence. My boy lay in the dirt. He looked dead — his atrophied, scarred limbs splayed out, unmoving. Had the demon taken my son's spirit to the underworld? That's what everyone was wondering. Was this the price paid for its eviction?

Yeshua ignored them, all His focus on my boy. He reached down and grabbed his hand. My son lifted his head. The crowd gasped. He fixed his eyes on Yeshua, clear of gaze. Yeshua's lips quirked up and He gave a tug. And my son ... who hadn't walked since... ever... folded one leg under his body, and levered himself up with the other. And he stood up. And they grinned at each other. Then they looked at me, and my son said, 'Abba!'

And I—I sat down suddenly in the dirt and cried like a baby. For I had received a miracle: my faithlessness had been met with divine condescension. I deserved nothing from God—but He gave anyway. Because love cares, and grace stoops.

# The Walls of Jericho

## ANNE HAMIILTON

The highest fortress hides
the deepest hurt,
the strongest tower defends
the darkest pain.
Thick walls, long-built, protect
the lonely heart
far out upon this scarred and barren plain.

Invincible these gates
to guile or stealth,
these stony parapets
are stormed in vain.
Hope's locked within, quite safe
from any lure.
Is there no chance we can build trust again?

If——
with seven-fold love,
I come patiently round –
and round, and round,
and patiently round –
and round, and round,
and patiently round –
will your walls,
My child,
come tumbling down?

# A Contemplative Prayer for a Victorious Man

## JUSTIN YEEND

# Day 1

## THE DEATH OF SELF

### GOOD FRIDAY 15 APRIL, 1992. 7PM

Rain falls from a dark and gloomy sky. A thunderstorm is expected at any moment. The speedometer on the 1980 Corona station wagon hits 100. Saul is looking forward to gatecrashing a local Christian gathering. No-one hates Christians more than he does. For a teenager like Saul, this is personal. His dark days of attending the Christian boarding school come flooding back as the rain pelts down on the windscreen. Saul feels a fire of anger ignite and burn inside him.

A landmark comes into view—Contemplation House.

Lightning strikes a White Gum. They don't call them widowmakers for nothing.

The tall tree falls across the road right in front of Saul's car. No time to swerve. His last words as the vehicle hits the tree at full impact—*'Jesus Christ.'*

Darkness engulfs Saul in the silence of the vehicle. Out of the darkness, a bright light appears. The light appears to be a man. But Saul can't see his face. The man seems to be everywhere, all at once. When the man speaks it is as if his voice reverberates heavily inside Saul's chest. Saul feels the voice as if it is both inside him and outside him at the same time.

The man says, *'Saul, why do you persecute me?'*

*'Who the hell are you?'* Saul responds.

*'I am Jesus, whom you are persecuting. Now get up and go to your destination. There you will find out what you need to do next.'*

The man disappears. As does everything else. All is pitch black. Saul drifts out of consciousness.

# THE DARK VOID

### EASTER SATURDAY 16 APRIL, 1992. 7PM

Saul wakes up. No vision. Blind as a bat.

He can feel the firmness of a bed mattress, the softness of bedsheets, and the cold metal of a bedrail. It's a noisy place, there are a lot of people around. One elderly voice at a distance calls out for a nurse.

Multiple voices, closer at the foot of his bed. They sound like doctors, reading off a series of observational data, physiological signs, and the outcomes of completed tests. The group moves closer, a tone of excitement and astonishment to their conversation. Phrases like… *'There is no evidence of physical trauma'* … and … *'We expect a full recovery'* … seem to levitate and glide through the air.

A doctor approaches and asks Saul a few basic questions. *'What is your age?'*

*'Nineteen.'*

*'What is the year?'*

*'Nineteen ninety-two,'* replies Saul.

*'We expect your vision to return shortly. It's likely only temporary. We'll keep you here a little longer for observation.'*

The time spent in pitch-black darkness has left Saul with time to reflect and a sense of lingering curiosity. The experience with the man claiming to be Jesus was so real. But Saul soon dismisses these thoughts. Perhaps the incident is a post-traumatic stress response. He is shaken, but grateful for his seemingly miraculous escape, wellbeing and recovery.

The doctors keep Saul in hospital another night for observation. They plan to discharge him later the following day when they expect his vision to be fully restored.

# Day 3

## A NEW BEGINNING

### EASTER SUNDAY 4 APRIL, 2021. 7AM

Saul wakes up.

He can feel the firmness of a bed mattress, the softness of bedsheets, and the cold metal of a bedrail. It's a noisy place. One voice, at a distance, possibly an elderly man, calls out for a nurse.

Déjà vu.

Saul has a partial visual impairment. A doctor approaches and asks a few basic questions to assess Saul's memory. He shakes his head as if he is not happy with the answers.

Saul explains that he recalls coming into hospital on Friday night following a car accident. The doctor informs Saul of the correct date. Saul quickly calculates his age—48 years old! Three key diagnostic words from the doctor hang in the air— *Severe Retrograde Amnesia.*

The doctor informs Saul that he was brought to hospital two days ago by a stranger called Sam. Sam had found Saul lying on a street corner near Contemplation House. The doctor explains that Australia is in the middle of a COVID-19 pandemic. The Chief Health Officer is about to announce a three-day lockdown very soon. Saul will need to be discharged to safe and secure accommodation where he can receive meals and support, and then followed up as an outpatient. Somewhat serendipitously, Sam works at Contemplation House where there is currently a vacancy. The doctor informs Saul that Sam can pick him up from the ward tomorrow morning and escort him to the accommodation. Saul begrudgingly agrees to this plan.

# Day 4

## TOURIST IN A FOREIGN LAND

### EASTER MONDAY 5 APRIL, 2021. 7PM

The car arrives at Contemplation House and Sam walks Saul inside. Once through the main door, they follow a corridor and into a large dining room. There is a large, long table in the centre with twelve men seated around it. The table is arranged like a banquet with an assortment of different foods. Saul is invited to sit with the other residents while Sam moves to the other side of the table and asks for silence. Sam says a prayer of thanks before starting the meal. Saul feels a growing sense of resentment. Two men on either side of him attempt to make conversation but Saul is not interested and becomes irritated by the religious banter. He stands up and looks down at the man sitting next to him. As the man glances up, Saul swings a strong fist at his head. The man falls to the floor. It feels good to let out his pent-up rage. But Saul's cathartic victory is short-lived. He is led away to a small room to contemplate. A radio announcement echoes in the hall—the city is about to go into a three-day lockdown from tomorrow.

# Day 5

## THE PILGRIM AWAKENS
### TUESDAY 6 APRIL, 2021. 7PM

The dark room focuses Saul's mind into deep reflection.

Trays of food remain on the floor, uneaten. Saul is hungry but cannot eat. His anger has consumed but not satisfied him.

As he sits on his bunk, a bright light appears. Memories flood his mind—all the events from the past 29 years. The person he has become is not the person he thought he was. After the car accident, the vision of Jesus had sparked his intellectual curiosity and interest in spirituality. Over almost three decades, Saul's identity evolved from atheist to agnostic and finally to spiritual but not religious. He was considered an expert in his field of Mindfulness Training. He had become quite wealthy, and his professional achievements were considered a victory both for himself and his peers.

Saul recalls having a celebratory meal with his colleagues on Maundy Thursday, 2021. Later that night, he had walked briskly past Contemplation House. It was raining heavily, and he had wanted to get to his car quickly. Looking up, he saw a vehicle speeding and swerving dangerously. It was hurtling towards him. He ducked into a dark alley to find both safety and cover from the rain. As the steep walls of the mountainous building loomed above, he heard a crash behind him.

Even in the dark, Saul recognised the distant features of a White Gum. They don't call them widowmakers for nothing.

Déjà vu.

An angry teenager exited the car—hurling profanities, something about Christians. Saul stumbled, falling towards a large pool of beautiful still water.

The next thing he remembered was waking up in the hospital on Easter Sunday.

# Day 6

## A DARK DAY OF THE SOUL
### WEDNESDAY 7 APRIL, 2021. 7AM

Saul sits down with Sam to reflect on his vision and the sudden return of his memory. Afterwards, they shake hands and Sam leads Saul out of the room into an extensive garden consisting of colourful plants, a fountain, and a water well at the centre. Saul joins the twelve men huddled together, sitting on the grass. They are discussing the story of Nicodemus in the Gospel of John.

Saul apologises to the man he hit on Monday. As he contemplates what it might mean to be born again, he notices another man standing in the dappled sunlight by the well. Saul has a mixed sense of curiosity and mild apprehension—simultaneously drawn to this man but unable to move forward and introduce himself. He feels himself overwhelmed by a dark cloud looming above his head. He falls to his knees and cries a cloudful of tears. As he glances upwards at the growing blackness of the cloud—it feels as if it has a life of its own, as if somehow the darkness has engulfed him. Immobilised by fear, anxiety, and grief, he feels a longing to connect with God.

Saul tries to say a prayer but cannot find the words. Yet he senses the space around him becoming quiet and still. Somehow, he knows he can rest in a Presence he doesn't understand. The vision fades as everything turns black.

Sam and some of the men lead Saul back to his room where he falls into a deep, peaceful sleep.

# Day 7

## GRACE AND REBIRTH

### THURSDAY 8 APRIL, 2021. 7AM

A dream unfolds as Saul drives along an empty desert road, making his way towards a parked car. Someone waits in the driver's seat. Although Saul wants to stop and engage, he feels a mix of apprehension and curiosity. He drives on. The road veers away, hugging the edge of an extremely steep mountain. Without warning, a striking artificial-looking bronze serpent appears directly in front of him. He is startled into wakefulness by a uniquely visceral jolt in his body. The remaining milliseconds of dream imagery occur in a kind of semi-alert state of consciousness. He jumps out of the vehicle and off the side of the mountain, but from a third-person perspective. It feels as if the decision to leap is outside of his control. Believing he had jumped to his death, Saul is astonished to find himself back in first-person view, paddling in a pool of beautiful still water. As he swims, he can see the parked car on the other side of the water. He feels an inexplicable draw toward the person in it.

Saul leaps from his bed and races to the garden. This pre-dawn space is empty of people, except for the man he had seen yesterday standing by the well and the fountain.

'Welcome back, Saul.' The man smiles, as he gently lays a hand on Saul's shoulder.

In this very moment, Saul experiences a spiritual quickening that burns like a fire in the pit of his stomach—he is Nicodemus. The man standing before him is Jesus Christ—his King and his Saviour.

The sound of a gentle breeze whistles throughout the garden. Nicodemus feels the soft wind move against his face. He asks, 'May I have a drink?'

Jesus draws a cup of water from the bucket in the well and hands it to him.

# Flame of Hope

## JENNY WOOLSEY

*J*ulie rocked herself in the love seat on her back deck, her hands wrapped around her cold coffee mug. She stared down at the garden, focusing on the shrivelled brown rose. That flower had once emanated a gorgeous fragrance—now it was nothing—just how she felt. Her vibrant spirit was crushed, her identity destroyed. The walls of her home, once a paradise, were now a prison walled by her husband, Greg.

Each morning and evening, Julie would open her Bible with its yellow fluoro-highlighted passages and handwritten notes in the margins to read about God's love for His people, His help in times of trouble. She read about Daniel's escape from the lions and Job's struggle with losing everything. She admired their strength and enduring faith. But even though the words reached out from the pages, in her heart she questioned… *If God really loves me, how could He let me marry this monster?* She'd asked Him if Greg was the chosen one. The shared interests, their faith, his family… and she thought, *Yes.*

'What are you wearing? That's see-through. You're not leaving the house in it.'

Julie frowned. She liked her new white loose-fitting cotton dress. Yes, it was a touch see-through in the sun, but it was cool and comfortable.

'Don't give me that look. Just do as I say.' He glared down at her. 'And make sure my dinner is left in the fridge for me. I'll be hungry after kickboxing.'

Julie nodded, tugging at the back of her curly hair. Once, she would have argued but, after eight years of losing, she remained silent.

At work, Julie told Sue, her teaching colleague, 'I can't go out with you. Greg won't let me.'

'Really? We're just going to a Folkart painting workshop. What does he think we're doing?' Sue crossed her arms.

'I know.'

'Have you ever thought about leaving him?' Sue's eyebrows furrowed. 'I'm saying this out of love. He isn't treating you right.'

'You're coming with me to my karate tournament in Toowoomba on the weekend.'

'But I have study to do. Can't you go on your own? My

assignment's due next week.' Julie was already struggling to get her Masters subject finished while working full-time.

'No, you're coming with me.' With that, Greg left the house, revved the engine of his red Subaru and squealed away.

Julie turned the TV volume up, so the neighbours couldn't hear her, and screamed, 'God, change him. I can't do this anymore!'

On Sunday, the congregation stood with their hands raised in praise. Julie would usually have joined them, but she stood hollow—like an old, burnt-out tree. Beside her, Greg moved his lips to the hymn. He wrapped his arm around her shoulders and pulled her to him. She smelt the cologne she'd once adored but now detested.

On the way out, Pastor Peter asked, 'How are you today, Julie?'

'She's fine.' Greg ran a hand through his permed hair.

Tears welled in Julie's eyes. She shook her head. The pastor glanced from Julie to Greg and then back again. 'Come and talk to me.'

She studied her sandals. Outside, Greg stuck to her like a piece of sticky tape—at the counter where she made them both a coffee, at the morning tea table where she chose a bunch of grapes and when she spoke to Deb. Still feeling hungry, Julie slid back to the table and chose a cupcake.

'Don't eat that,' he hissed. 'You'll get fat.'

Julie looked around. 'How about you go and say hi to George. He's standing over there by himself.'

'No.'

'Brett's over there.'

'No.' Greg's dark brown eyes pierced hers. Julie knew from that look there was no chance of speaking to Peter.

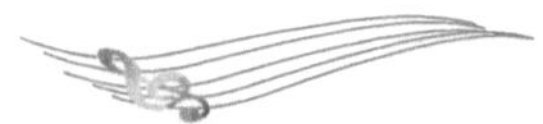

Breathless, Julie just made it to the landline. 'Hello.'

'Hi Julie, it's Pastor Peter here. Is now a good time to talk?'

Julie's heart skipped. Greg wasn't due home for an hour. 'Yes.'

'I was concerned about you on Sunday. Can you tell me what's happening?'

Tears filled Julie's eyes and she blinked them away. She sucked in the air and an explosion of words erupted. Apart from a few, 'ahas' and 'mmms', Peter just listened. Julie sagged down into a dining room chair, rested her forehead on her hand and sobbed.

After a moment of silence, Peter said, 'Let's get you into marriage counselling. I will talk to Greg. It's going to be okay. God can change him.'

A small flame of hope lit in Julie's gut.

Julie listened from the loungeroom as Peter spoke to Greg on the phone.

'She's making a mountain out of a molehill.'

'Why?'

'Yeah, okay.'

*Click.*

Chills consumed Julie as if she was standing naked in the snow. She dared not move. Greg found her, his fists clenched. 'Why do I have to go to marriage counselling? Just because you don't like being told what to do. It says in the Bible that a wife must obey her husband.'

'Because… I… can't… do… this… anymore.'

'Ha! It's in your head.'

That night Julie knelt beside her bed and prayed, 'Pastor Peter said You can change him. He said You'd changed Pastor Evan who used to be like Greg. Please change him. I can't do this for much longer.'

The fragrance of lavender wafted through the marriage counsellor's office. Julie and Greg were directed to sit on the three-seater fabric couch. The counsellor introduced herself as Margaret.

'It's not me, it's her.' Greg shook his head and cracked his knuckles. 'I've done nothing wrong.'

Julie pulled her knees up and hugged them. Greg lay sprawled out on the other end like a lanky praying mantis.

'God can change him,' Margaret told her on their way out. 'Pray and believe.'

As the counselling sessions continued, Greg was a granite boulder baking in the summer sun while Julie's empty candleholder filled with black depression. 'You're not leaving me,' Greg threatened on the way home after the third session, the wedge between them clearly visible. 'If you go, I'm coming after you. No one else can have you.'

Isolated from her friends and masking how controlling Greg was when she spoke to her family, Julie sunk lower and lower. There had been no improvement in the marriage. The abuse continued. In Julie's mind, there was no light, no hope. That small flame of optimism she had at the first counselling session had long since been snuffed out.

Julie's mind entered an abyss. 'He's not going to change … He doesn't want to … And I can't leave him. I'm a Christian and I married him until death do us part … So I guess it will be death do us part.' Seeing suicide as the only means of escape, Julie set about investigating what pills she would need to end her life.

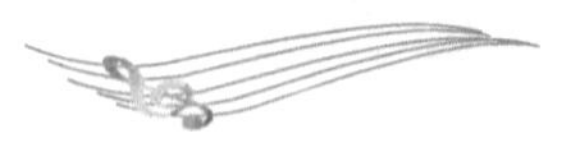

The next counselling session began as the others had. 'This is a waste of time,' Greg muttered. 'She's the problem, not me. I keep telling you that it's all in her crazy mind.'

Margaret, not taking sides, looked at him. She pushed a strand of grey hair behind her ear. 'What are you doing over the holidays?' she asked Julie.

In a week's time, the winter school holiday began. Greg would be working. 'Um, nothing. But do you think it would be okay for me to go home for the weekend?' Julie didn't know where that question had come from but now it was out. She leant forward, her eyes sending a silent plea to the counsellor.

'Yes, that sounds like a wonderful idea.' Margaret smiled.

'No.' Greg crossed his arms. 'Definitely not.'

Julie willed Margaret to keep going.

'I really think that would be a wise move. Give Julie a break.'

Greg glared from one woman to the other. 'Okay, but just for the weekend.'

The next evening, when Greg was at kickboxing training and the sun was dipping below the horizon, painting the sky in shades of pink and purple, Julie phoned her parents. 'Can I please come home for the weekend?'

Her dad sounded concerned. 'Yes, of course. What's wrong?'

'I'll explain when I get there. '

Thursday night came and Julie sat on the cold tiles of the shower cubicle, broken. Tears streamed down her cheeks. 'Please God, if he's not going to change, help me escape from this hell.'

As she prayed, the small flame of hope reignited.

On Friday afternoon Julie filled a suitcase, ensuring she packed her favourite Christian music CDs, her warm-like-a-hug chunky jumper and two pairs of comfortable jeans.

Saturday morning arrived. Her husband grudgingly started the car. 'I don't think you should be going.'

Julie stared at her fidgeting hands.

'I'll come and get you on Monday.'

Julie remained quiet as she stared out the side window, while Greg drove erratically up the highway to her parent's house.

The small flame of hope that had been lit in the shower flickered a little brighter. An escape plan was forming in her mind.

Her parents answered the doorbell.

'I'll be back on Monday afternoon.' Greg stood with his driver's door open.

Julie turned her back on him and scooted inside. Her father locked the door behind her.

The walls of Julie's childhood home wrapped around her like a safe, snug cocoon. In the loungeroom, her parents' eyes were a kaleidoscope of love, questions and worry. Julie collapsed into the recliner rocker and tears sprang from her eyes. Sobs wracked her body as she rocked back and forth.

Her father pulled her up and hugged her tight. It was a long time before words came from her lips but, after they did, all of the abuse and pain and suffering lay bare.

'We didn't know,' her mother said.

Julie nodded. She knew she'd been good at keeping up the façade.

'You are not going back to that treatment.' Her father handed her a tissue.

Julie nodded. The flame grew a little taller and brighter.

'God, now I have to tell him I'm not going back unless he changes. Help me!' she prayed.

It was Sunday afternoon. Julie picked up the telephone in the loungeroom. Her hands trembled. She stared at the crocheted white wedding bells with their red ribbon bows in the cabinet under the phone. Her mother had made them. It had been a beautiful wedding nine years earlier but the honeymoon had begun with a fight. She shook her head. She needed to do this. Julie dialled her home number, fear grabbing her like a deer caught in a trap. She so wanted to hang up.

'Hello.'

'I'm not coming back until you change.' Julie's voice was a trembling whisper.

'Yes, you are. I'm coming to get you.'

Julie took a deep breath. 'No, I'm staying here until you change.'

There was a long pause. 'Alright, if you need longer, I'll give you a week. Then I'm coming to get you.'

Julie's legs buckled as she placed the phone in its cradle.

Her dad encased her in his arms. 'You're not going back.'

Greg tried to win her back. Bunches of roses, Mickey Mouse toys and a sorry letter arrived.

Julie was torn. Was he changing? 'Maybe I should go back.' She nervously rubbed her hands together.

'Do you really want to? Do you think he has changed?' Sherry, her childhood friend, sat opposite her in the booth at the local takeaway.

Julie ordered a burger with the works and a thickshake — something she would never have done with Greg. 'I don't know. I asked him if he'd quit kickboxing for me and he said no.'

'I think you should stay with your parents until he can prove to you that he has changed.'

The week stretched into another week which then stretched into another week. Greg's messages, 'You're the problem. I'm not changing. I'm doing nothing wrong,' forced Julie to have the strength to stay firm. She continued to pray and to read her Bible.

Julie divorced Greg and the healing began. She felt free but a question kept spiralling in her mind. She needed answers. 'Does God forgive me for divorcing him? I married for better or worse, till death do us part.'

Alan, the community pastor, put down his cup of tea. Opening his Bible, he read, 'This is Ephesians 5:25–30... *a man should love his wife as Christ loved the church and gave Himself up for her... Husbands ought to love their wives as their own bodies...'*

Julie hugged herself.

'He did not love you that way and that's not what God wanted for you.' Alan's eyes were warm like hot chocolate with marshmallows.

Tears filled Julie's eyes.

'Also, think about love. In 1 Corinthians 13 it says that love is kind… it does not dishonour others… nor delight in evil... Did he treat you with love?'

She shook her head and whispered, 'Thank you.'

Many years later, urged by a psychologist, Julie wrote a letter to Greg, pouring sentences after sentence out of her heart, filling multiple pages. She told him how he had hurt her, she reminisced about the good times and expelled the painful trauma. She finished with words of sincere forgiveness.

Through therapy and prayer, Julie learned to dismantle her destructive thought patterns and internalise what the Bible said about how God saw her… She was a victor, not a victim. She was strong and courageous. She could do all things through Christ who gave her strength… and God really loved her.

Julie forged on with her new life and family. Sometimes, in the quiet moments, she would reflect on where she'd come from. That broken woman, lost in the darkness, crying out to God and yearning for the trauma to stop had become a woman with the promise of brighter days. She clothed herself in the armour of a mighty warrior and now carried her brightly-shining flame of hope for all to see.

# Lonely Old Guitar
## MIRANDA DE JAGER

*O* the dust, the ever-increasing dust,
 obstructing my view through the attic window.
My only view to the outside world,
is getting hazier by the day.
Just a lonely old guitar...
I can't remember the last time,
I felt the strumming of sensitive fingers,
and accurately timed pressure on my neck.

O, the beautiful music I produced.
University sounded so exciting,
but I was not good enough—
Patrick did not take his old guitar.

For the first time in many years,
I hear the attic door squeaking,
a familiar female voice humming a lovely tune.
Has the dust affected my vision?
No, it really is Cindy, but she's changed.
What a beautiful lady she's become!
That's right, pick up this lonely old guitar.
She takes me out and down the stairs.

O, how good it feels to be cleaned.
Well, young lady, I do like sitting on your knee.
Her hands are soft and gentle,
but I sound terrible—that's not me!

You have to tune me first, my dear,
but, she doesn't seem to hear...
We won many competitions, Patrick and I,
that is, after he'd learned to play.
Will I go through the process again?
The false notes, and complaints about sore fingers,
or is Cindy just fooling around?
Would she really learn to play
this lonely old guitar?

But then she puts me down and walks away.
I hear noises—is that Patrick's voice?
He enters the room and picks me up.
My heart rejoices as he tunes me and strokes my
strings.

Patrick's familiar baritone voice
mingles with Cindy's soprano harmony.
They sing: *Amazing Grace, how sweet the sound,*
and I feel a tear dripping on my back.
Patrick wipes it away as Cindy touches his arm.
Wow, I didn't know I could still sound so good!
And a Christian song—that's a first…
Cindy smiles and says: I'm so glad you found God,
It's an answer to our prayers.

I sense a new peace in Patrick as he hands me to
Cindy.
He smiles: 'Thanks for cleaning him, sis, he's yours
now.'
Cindy hugs us both with joy and says:
Thank you, bro, you'll need to teach me though.

# Epistle

## LINDA BARTON

My Darling Rain Cloud,

It is almost the end of winter and I have not seen you for many months. I am so sorry for telling you to 'go away!' I pray you will find it in your heart to forgive me and come back. I did not mean it when I said you cast a grey pall over my existence and your constant weeping wore me down and eroded my faith. I wish I could retract those sentiments that made you withdraw.

Baby, I miss you so very much. My life is a desert without you. I lie out in the fiery heat of the midday sun, barren and desolate. The heavens over me are bronze and my heart is turning to iron. I am an empty vessel without you and I thirst every day for your companionship. My lips, parched and cracked, long for the touch of your sweet moist kiss. I am exhausted with longing and I ache with my body and soul for your return. I beseech you not to forsake me. Don't let my pleas disintegrate into dust.

My love, you bring life and colour to my world. I lie awake at night and recall how my heart leapt like a tree frog every time I saw you; how alive and refreshed I feel when we embrace. I stare up at the stars and remember the rhythmic sound of your voice, like the tinkling of piano keys. Music to my ears.

My dearest, we have always been together. God joined us and decreed we should never be parted. I think back to all the times we have shared and all our laughter and tears. Since time began, we have enjoyed a satisfying and fruitful relationship. So, my love, I hope and pray to the heavens above you will come back to me.

Yours forever,

*Dry Earth*

# The Coin

## TERRY GATFIELD

*My* good friend Benson is getting on a bit and starting to notice the changes that come with aging. This is especially true with regard to his physical abilities, yet, he has still retained most of his mental faculties and has kept a sharp, enquiring mind. However, a recent occurrence challenged that notion.

Benson walks daily to keep his body fit, and to focus on the mind and soul. He loves the tranquillity of local parklands, the silence of the trees as well as the birdsong and the music of the trickling water of the walkway creek after the spring showers.

His canine friend, a Border Collie named Ray, always accompanies him on his walks. They are a faithful couple and adore each other. No leads or collars are needed—they read each other's minds. Benson behaves and so does Ray. But one day, Ray unexpectedly disappeared.

'Here, Ray.' No response. Benson backtracked and searched the creek. There was Ray with his tail in the air as his front paws dug in the gravel bed.

'Sit. Drop.'

Ray dropped. His bright knowing eyes seemed to say, 'Look what I discovered.'

It was a round piece of dirty metal about the diameter of a matchbox—flat on one side but with raised markings on the other. The metal glowed in the shade of the overhanging rainforest tree; an aura seemed to surround it. Benson picked it up. Warm to the touch and rather large, it was, however, light.

Intrigued, Benson took his new treasure home to inspect with the aid of chemicals and a scrubbing brush. However clean, it did not give up its secret. The three symbols on the front were clear but their sense was difficult to decipher. The back was a dark bronze-like material; the front was clearly silver. Was it an ancient coin, a type of token, a magic charm or simply an item of jewellery? He did sense was that it was special, had to be respected and that its voice was waiting to be discovered.

For want of a better word, Benson just called his find 'the coin'. He made a leather pouch to keep it safe, attaching a thin leather thong to hang it around his neck. That pouch never left him. At night, he slept with it under his pillow. It gave him great comfort and a feeling of warmth. Benson even imagined the coin gave him supernatural protection.

Friends' guesswork couldn't throw any light on it. They became frustrated with his never-ending search to untangle the mystery so Benson sought out individuals who would take him more seriously.

His first choice was a skilled musician and profound thinker named Shamus, nicknamed 'Steinway Shamus' due to his skill on the piano. He had spent many years studying the formation of western music derived from Greek and Roman times and from the 13th century. He claimed to possess an original music score of one of Vivaldi's Baroque masterpieces. When Shamus saw the coin he noted that the first character was shaped like a musical minim. He spent days examining ancient music scores to see if there was a reasonable fit with the other mystery characters that preceded the minim, but exhausted his vast library of manuscripts. Shamus could not solve the mystery and suggested Benson seek another solution.

Not daunted, Benson sought the advice of a faithful friend, a vivacious and elegant lady, Hanna. Her passion and encyclopaedic knowledge were the study of ancient Hebrew Biblical texts, and especially the Dead Sea Scrolls. Perhaps the last character was the Hebrew 'Daleth' equivalent to our letter D or maybe 'Resh' which we understand to be our letter R. It was a start but proved a futile journey. Shaking her head, Hanna suggested Dinita, an Egyptologist specialising in hieroglyphics might solve the riddle of the coin.

Dinita was a charming lady full of grace, wisdom and insight. She had worked for years on the tomb of Tutankhamun. She compared the coin's symbols with Egyptian hieroglyphics. However her extensive knowledge and insight also failed to find any promising leads.

Benson took up an interest in coin-collecting. The world through the ages had developed all kinds of currencies and tokens as mediums of exchange. Australian catalogues revealed nothing of any significance regarding Benson's coin. In desperation, he travelled to the world-famous Rochette Money Museum in Colorado Springs, USA. There he was introduced to Marcus, an extraordinary man who had developed the technique of palming a coin with his right hand while caressing the coin with his left-hand fingers—then, without looking, he could tell you the country of origin, the date, the monarch, if there was one, the mintage of that year and the approximate market value of the coin. Marcus, perhaps for the first time in his life, drew a blank.

Benson was not too disturbed—he and the coin had become close companions. They seemed to be able to talk to each other—perhaps like young children talking to their favourite teddy bear. The quest to unravel the mystery continued. Was it some type of medieval charm? He didn't consider it had any negative, evil or sinister connotations. Was it a ceremonial item used by an ancient culture in some kind of celebration?

An old friend named Hazelly had made an intense study of African tribal costumes and culture in the domain of religious ceremonies. She took charge of the coin for a number of days, as 'I need to meditate to hear the voice.' A few days later she returned to Benson saying, 'I am sorry, I have no voice to share. The answer may lie with Clifton the Wizard.'

Clifton was no stranger to Benson as he lived fairly close in the huge hollow of a magnificent cedar tree, deep in the rainforest. He was a kind of hobbit. No one knew his age. He was loved and always had time for anybody and everybody. He could always be found close to his log fire along with a large pot of tea. Although he had the nickname 'Wizard' there was no magic or sorcery about him. He was renowned for his deep contemplative spirit and for being a lover of nature. Clifton found simple understandings and solutions to the most complex and mysterious things in life.

'Why didn't I think to consult Clifton before?' Benson fumed.

At daybreak, Clifton's customary pot of tea was ready, and he offered a plate of hot duck sausages and fresh bread for breakfast. Benson unfolded the full story of the coin. 'I have a pressing need to find some closure after long months of searching.'

Clifton shut his eyes, held the coin close to his chest and chewed his bread. Opening his eyes, he said, 'That is wonderful, but I cannot see the problem.'

Clifton held the coin upside down between his index finger and thumb.

The marks he'd sought so long to understand were three English letters: *L J P*.

Clifton spoke in beautiful dulcet tones. 'The three letters obviously stand for Love, Joy, Peace—the first three of the Fruit of the Holy Spirit. You and your colleagues may have been misled by the small notch on the outside rim of the coin. It should point downwards not upwards. The Fruit of the Spirit comes down to us. It is grounded. It is grounded in us. We have to transform our thinking and at times turn something through 180 degrees to see it more clearly. My dear Benson, what a precious thing you have found. Cherish it and let Love, Joy and Peace flow in and through you.'

Enigma solved and rest beckoned. Benson left that day filled with LJP.

# A Future Promise

## KAREN ROPER

Shafts of red dawnlight slanted into the room and, as Hannah dozed between sleeping and waking, she wondered what day it was. 'Oh, that's right. It's the day to pack up and go to the feast.'

She thought of all the things she needed to gather for the overnight journey to Shiloh. Clothes, food, blankets—and perhaps an extra lamb for the sacrifice. At least today's preparations would keep her mind off her problems. Actually, *problem*, singular. She really had only one— she was childless. Barren. The shame and gossip in her community often felt intolerable.

She knew her husband loved her. Still, it was sometimes hard to feel Elkanah's affection when she had to share him with another woman—a wife who'd already given him a trove of children. If she let herself dwell on the situation too long, she'd sink into sadness again. And that was beginning to be a daily occurrence.

In her deepest, uneasiest ponderings, she wondered if God was somehow punishing her. But she couldn't think of anything so big that His grace would be denied to her. She considered His commandments one by one. She loved God and was good to others, she always dutifully kept the Sabbath day and attended each of the feasts throughout the year. Yet, when she prayed, all she heard from God was a whisper, 'Wait!'

At least it wasn't *no*. But hadn't she waited long enough already? Flinging aside the depressing question, she forced herself to get up and make breakfast. Lots to do and little time to do it.

The meal was a sombre affair. Even the children were quiet for once. It was Elkanah's job to prepare the donkeys and select a lamb for the sacrifice. She thought of asking him about an extra one but the silence was stifling. All Peninnah, the other wife, had to do was ready the children. Everything else was left to Hannah.

After breakfast, Hannah prepared the food, packed her clothing and all the bedding. She prepared some fine flour and sweet, aromatic spices for the sacrifice.

A few hours later, the bedrolls had been tied to the donkeys and the food in the saddlebags. Peninnah and her children mounted the pair of animals and, with a kick to their sides, set off for Shiloh. Elkanah followed them, the lamb over his shoulders. Hannah preferred to walk anyway. So she strolled down the dusty road, chatting to the other women from their village who were also making their way to the feast.

After catching up on all the news from each family, small talk of crops, recipes and weather took over. They stayed with Elkanah's cousin overnight, sleeping on his roof under the stars. Hannah was reminded of God's promise to Abraham and his childless wife Sarah: *Can you count the stars? So shall your descendants be.*

*And mine?* She couldn't help but wonder. Flickers of hope warmed her heart.

They arrived at Shiloh late the next day and settled into the lodgings Elkanah had arranged on their last visit.

The next morning they all went to the Tabernacle for the yearly sacrifice. It was a joyous time of remembering what God had done for them, feasting and enjoying the provision and protection of God. But Hannah was overcome with sadness.

When it came time for Elkanah to give his offering, he gave a portion to Peninnah and to each of her children, but to Hannah he gave a double amount. She knew she should feel loved and appreciated. And for a moment, she did.

But once Elkanah left to talk to the other men, Peninnah taunted her. 'I have no idea what's wrong with you. You can't even give Elkanah sons. Look at all my children. I am so blessed and you are not. Yet he gives you the double portion.'

In an instant, Hannah's mood changed. She felt rejected, unloved and unwanted. *Why, oh, why has God forgotten me?* She turned away, trying to hide the tears.

Elkanah was by her side. 'Why are you crying? Am I not better to you than ten sons?'

Hannah couldn't answer. She loved Elkanah very much, but her life and her arms felt empty without a baby.

The only place she'd felt any solace was in the Tabernacle. It was only a short walk away. When she arrived, she pulled the curtains aside and went into the outer court. Nobody was there. She sighed with relief. *They're all at the feast.*

Bowing down and rocking back and forward, she poured out her heart to God, more desperately than ever before. 'Oh Lord of Hosts, why have You forgotten me? I have been married for a long time but still I have no child. Please heal me, God. Please forgive me, God. Why oh, why?'

Hannah had prayed similar prayers on many occasions but, this time, she felt a change in her heart. *What if I give my child to God?* She sniffed and wiped away a track of tears. *Where did that thought even come from? Would God really expect me to give up a child He has given me?* Yet, as she considered the idea, it settled into her heart, bringing a strange peace. *Is this the answer I have been seeking for years? Does God have a special purpose for my child? Is this the reason I have been left waiting?*

Perhaps God was not angry or indifferent to her. Perhaps her motives were wrong. She was selfishly asking for a child so she could know that her husband loved her, even though he said he did. She wanted a son to stop Peninnah's biting criticism and the town's pity. Yet, was it that God somehow had a higher purpose for her, and she'd been so upset, she couldn't see it? Hannah wrestled with the thought of surrendering the child she longed for so deeply. Then finally she whispered, 'Yes, Lord of Hosts, if that is Your will, that is what I will pray.'

As soon as she spoke, she realised the child of the promise should be a Nazarite: dedicated to the Lord. *No shaving or hair-cutting. No wine.* So she made a vow, mouthing the words in silence. 'O Lord of Hosts, if You will indeed look on the affliction of Your maidservant and remember me, and not forget Your maidservant, but will give Your maidservant a male child, then I will give him to the Lord all the days of his life, and no razor shall come upon his head.'

Footsteps echoed behind her. *Isn't everyone else at the feast?* She straightened herself and stopped rocking and turned around, coming face to face with the priest Eli. She braced herself—he was so lenient with his sons, he never stopped their abuse of others, but that didn't mean he would tolerate her. *Should I even be in here now?* But she desperately needed to plead with God.

Eli spoke sternly to her. 'How long will you be drunk? Put your wine away from you.'

Hannah stared. She didn't know whether to cry or be offended. Was he such a hypocrite that he'd admonish her but not his own sons? But she remembered he was a man of God and maybe, just maybe, he could help even if he was angry with her. She lowered her head and spoke humbly. 'No, my lord. I am a woman of sorrowful spirit. I have drunk neither wine nor intoxicating drink but have poured out my soul toward the Lord.' When he didn't comment, she went on, 'Do not consider your maidservant a wicked woman, for out of the abundance of my grief I have spoken until now.'

She waited. Was he going to throw her out of the Tabernacle? What would happen next? As the silence lengthened, she became scared and uncertain.

At last Eli spoke. 'Go in peace, and the God of Israel grant your petition which you have asked of Him.'

Hannah sighed in relief. He didn't banish her but blessed her. He gave her a Word from God! A promise she could hold onto. *Surely if the priest said that God would grant my petition, He will.* 'Let your maidservant find favour in your sight.'

Hannah burst into song. She left the Tabernacle, rejoicing. Surely this time God had heard her prayer. Thinking back over the encounter, Hannah couldn't believe how frightened she'd been of the priest. Yet he'd given her a blessing. This was a sign from God. But how would she ever give up her promised son? That was something to ponder on and work through another day.

Hannah returned to the lodgings Elkanah had hired. The day was almost over. He was watching and waiting for her. No Peninnah to be seen. She must be still at the feast.

'Where have you been?' Elkanah's eyes showed his worry. 'I was just about to go out looking for you.' He tilted his head, quirking an eyebrow. 'You look happy. What's happened?'

'I am sorry.' Even the remorse Hannah felt couldn't burst her bubble of joy. 'I needed to get away by myself for a while. I'm better now.' She didn't want to explain more than that, not now.

She retired early, pondering on the amazing day she'd had. She truly felt a bubbling joy that she hadn't felt since the day of her betrothal to Elkanah. A smile played with her lips as she fell asleep.

The joy didn't diminish on the long walk home. Nor even over the next week as Elkanah caught up on the chores that had built up in their absence. She noticed his glance when he thought she wasn't looking. There was a rustling at her curtain one evening. Elkanah was there. 'Hannah.' His voice seemed gentler, more loving. 'We haven't spent much time together lately. I have been busy, too busy. And I have missed you. Let's spend the night together?'

She welcomed him, as eager as a young bride. It was true he'd been busy. Even Peninnah had complained. But what was she doing, thinking of her rival at a time like this?

The next morning Hannah arose first and came back with water and some bread for Elkanah. The time was right to share with him what had transpired in the Tabernacle on the day of the feast—now, before he set off for work.

A shout interrupted her before she even began. 'Elkanah ben Jeroham!' A messenger had come from another village to say he was needed urgently.

Hannah's bubble of joy was squelched with momentary disappointment. She'd have to wait until the evening to spill her secret. But he did not come home that night. Nor for many days. Even after he returned, he didn't elaborate on why he'd been summoned with such urgency. But he was busier than ever. There was never a time to be alone with him and reveal God's promise to them.

A month went by. Hannah woke one morning and vomited. The bubble of joy burst. She struggled up, dizzy with nausea, and tried to carry out her chores. By midday, the feeling passed and she felt sure she was better. But the next morning, she was ill again. And the next. And the next.

Even Elkanah, busy as he was, noticed. She could see his concern about her tiredness and her lack of appetite. Peninnah took to staring at her in an uncomfortable way. She was used to the taunts but this was different. Peninnah kept frowning as if she was suspicious. *Does she think I'm pretending?*

Then, one morning, Peninnah confronted her. 'Hannah, are you with child?'

Hannah blinked, astonished. She hurried back behind her curtain and threw herself on the bed. *Is that why I feel so sick? When was the last time I had my cycle? Months back.*

Hannah cried. Her prayer had been answered. *Finally.* God had miraculously opened her womb, and she bubbled with the realisation she was with child. She must tell Elkanah. He hadn't yet heard the story of what had happened in the Tabernacle at the feast.

Hannah hurried out to the fields where Elkanah was working. She heard a yell, 'Your wife is coming, Elkanah!'

Elkanah threw down his tools and ran to meet her. 'What's wrong, Hannah?'

She laughed. 'We are with child.'

Elkanah roared with delight and threw his arms around her. Then they both wept, overjoyed. Elkanah walked Hannah back home and instructed Peninnah to care for her and keep her safe. Hannah was surprised to realise Peninnah was happy for her, though a little jealous flicker emerged from time to time.

Months later, Hannah's prayers were fully answered when she gave birth to a baby boy. 'God heard me,' she said, and so she named him Samuel.

Hannah had trusted in the Lord through all her hardships. She had prayed and then believed in the word that Eli the priest had given her.

After Samuel was weaned, Hannah did indeed give him to God. She took him to the Tabernacle and left him there in the care of Eli the priest. Samuel grew up and became a great prophet and restorer in Israel. He was the one God had chosen to heal the nation after the calamity brought on by the violence of the sons of Eli.

'Wait!' God had said to her.

When He says the same to us, we should follow her example, praying and trusting in Him.

# A Double Blessing

## RAELENE PURTILL

*To all who mourn in Israel,*
*He will give a crown of beauty for ashes,*
*a joyous blessing instead of mourning.*

*Isaiah 61:3* NLT

'I can't wake her.'

'She's just playing. Let me try.' My husband disappeared behind the curtain dividing the room where our daughter lay. Three days before, Talitha complained of a headache, refused to eat and went to bed. When I looked in later that evening, she appeared to be sleeping easily. Yet by morning her body was warm, too warm even for this summer heat, and her breathing was strained and uneven. Some torment had her fidgeting and sweating. I stood and prayed by her bed, pleading with God for my little girl's life.

When Jairus found me, I was curled up on the floor, my face wet, my eyes exhausted from crying. Now, I hovered outside the curtain as though it were the impenetrable veil in the Temple, separated from the life of my daughter. Anxiety expanded the rhythm of my heartbeat. I was losing my breath. When Jairus emerged, the colour had left his face. His eyes were shadows above his pale cheeks. He shook his head and took my hand. 'I am sorry I doubted you, Abigail. Talitha is very sick. I am the head of our house but I don't know what to do.'

We held each other and he prayed. When he let me go, his face was flushed, and his eyes were bright. 'I know,' he declared. 'The teacher is in town. I will find Jesus. He will come.' He was out the door before I had time to process what he had said.

I returned to Talitha's bedside and continued my useless ministrations, wiping her forehead and holding her clammy hand. I remembered better days when she was healthy, running and playing with the children of the village. Her life filled my thoughts. The heat in the room lulled me to sleep until my mother-in-law, Deborah, put her head around the curtain. She put her hand on Talitha's forehead as soon as she entered. 'Jairus told me. Do you really think the teacher will come here to help a child?'

'We have heard of others. That is why Jairus has gone to see him.'

She rolled her eyes, clicked her tongue and left the room. I followed her out. She went to the fire and prepared some food, then encouraged me to eat. I agreed, but only to keep the peace.

'There is nothing more you can do.' She presented me with a bowl of meat and bread. 'If she doesn't get better, I will bring the doctor.'

'Jairus will return with the teacher.' I was trying to convince myself all would be well very soon.

Deborah shook her head. 'That man is trouble. My son should know better. He is the leader of the synagogue and he should not be going in search of this so-called rabbi.'

I pushed the unfinished bowl away and returned to Talitha. That was when I could not hear her breathing. 'Talitha, wake up!' I screamed as though I was shouting over a storm. 'Talitha!' I gathered her up and rocked her, the rhythm merging with my grief. I buried my head against hers and smelled her hair as though she were an infant. I sensed the life departing from her.

I became aware of a murmur outside the room. Deborah spoke clearly to our servant. 'Find your master. Tell him not to bother that teacher. Tell him Talitha has died.' Her voice was calm, as though it were an ordinary errand and she was organising the day as usual. On my side of the curtain, chaos prevailed. My mind was battered between despair and denial. I heard the scrape of the door against the floor as the servant departed. Then it seemed there were still others in our house.

'You can go in now,' I heard Deborah say.

The mourners removed Talitha's body from my arms and laid her on the cot. They wrapped her up with cold efficiency then, moving like shadows, took up their positions around her. The ritual lament began, accompanied by the moaning of a pipe and the beat of a frame drum. Their death worship surrounded me, and I could easily have fallen into the pit of hell myself, never to return. These black shadows were drawing out my will to live, extracting a scream from deep within me, I did not recognise the voice as my own. I staggered from their presence.

My vision was blurred by grief, so I wasn't sure what I was looking at, but the crowd became clearer as it approached. I recognised Jairus. He ran ahead and when he hugged me, my heart broke again, but he was almost jubilant. He took my face in his hands. 'There is hope.'

'No, my love. Talitha … our little girl …' I couldn't go on.

'I found the teacher. I have seen him heal already today. Everything will be alright.'

He took me in his arms again and, from over his shoulder, I thought I recognised a woman. There were many faces in the crowd surging behind the teacher, but this one appeared to be different—well, at least different from when I had last seen her. 'Is that Rachel?'

'Yes.' Jairus' face lit up. 'That's what I meant when I said I've seen Him heal already today.'

He beckoned my friend to join me and left us to our reunion while he showed the teacher into the house. Rachel smiled. I couldn't remember the last time that had happened. Ten years? No, it must be more. Talitha was twelve and Rachel's debilitating condition had started around the time she was born.

'Hello, Abigail.' Her eyes became sombre. 'I was so sorry to hear of your loss.'

I nodded. 'Thank you, but you … look at you. You are standing upright. I had forgotten how tall you are.'

She laughed, a light tinkling sound which floated above my grief. I sighed, but did not want to deny her the joy she expressed.

'After all these years, I have been healed. Jesus has healed me. You must go to your daughter now. We will talk later.'

We turned for the door, but before we could go in the mourners spilled out into the street. 'He thinks she's only sleeping,' one mocked. 'I have been in this business long enough to know the difference.' Minutes ago, this mourner had been chanting and moaning as she beat out the death rhythm.

'What does that itinerant preacher know anyway?' agreed another.

'Do you think we will still get paid?' A third one caught up to them and the trio lingered in the street outside our house as the rest of the mourners emerged.

Rachel and I went to the door only to be stopped by my mother-in-law. Deborah pointed, and in a sharp voice said, 'That woman cannot come in here.'

'She's my friend.'

'And I'm Talitha's bubbe. I know who this outcast is.' She folded her arms and scowled. 'You stay away.' Huffing, she returned inside.

Rachel touched my arm. 'She has done her part for tradition. I've had twelve years to get used to it. Go to your family.'

I squeezed Rachel's hand as if the years she spoke of had never been. 'Wait here.' My mind raced as I returned to Talitha's room. Why had Rachel been healed while my daughter had died? Why had Jairus witnessed that miracle while our own need for one had been overlooked?

Deborah was leaving. 'That so-called teacher has dismissed us all.' As she passed me, she snapped at the servant who tried to assist her. 'I don't need help. I can walk alone.'

In Talitha's room only Jairus, myself, the teacher and a few of his disciples remained. The shroud enfolding my daughter had been pulled back and her face was exposed. I bent to cover her again.

'Don't,' said Jairus.

'She's only sleeping,' said the teacher.

Our eyes met across my daughter's body. 'Is that why you sent the mourners out, because she is only sleeping? Is that why you stopped to heal Rachel, because our daughter was only sleeping?' My voice rose with each question until my throat constricted with a sob.

Jairus put his arm around me. I almost pushed him away, but not quite. I gripped his hand for support when my knees buckled. Jairus addressed the teacher by name. 'Jesus, I believe You can heal our child, my family, and that Your power comes from the Almighty.'

Somewhere deep down I believed that too. I wanted to believe but I was drowning in my grief and confusion.

'Little girl, wake up. Do not be afraid.' He addressed Talitha but He spoke directly to me with words that banished my fear, soothed my anger, and censured my grief.

Our daughter's eyes fluttered open and she squinted in the light, then gasped. Jairus knelt by the cot and hugged her. I froze until Jesus' words released me. 'Get her something to drink.'

'Of course.' I skipped out with joy propelling my feet. When I returned Jesus was in solemn discussion with Jairus.

'You must not tell anyone of this,' said the healer.

'But why not?' I interrupted.

He never did answer my question but put a finger to His lips in a gesture of silence. With quiet gratitude we showed Him and His disciples from the house. The crowd outside moved off as soon as Jesus joined them. One of the men with Him raised a hand in farewell before catching up.

'Who was that?' I asked.

'Matthew.' Jairus waved back.

'Wasn't he the —'

'Tax collector, yes.' He looked at me. 'Jesus has changed everything for us too, Abigail. We were mourning, but now our joy shines like morning light.'

I nodded. 'And I have my friend returned to me too. A double blessing.'

We joined Rachel at the table inside. 'You must forgive me,' I said to her as we settled.

'Then we shall forgive each other. It was my own desperation that delayed Jesus. I was running out of hope. There was nothing left for me but to grab hold of His power, to take it. At least you and Jairus were polite enough to ask His favour.' A brief smile touched her lips before she turned to watch Talitha play with Deborah.

'He would have been the same age,' she whispered.

'Oh, I'm so sorry.' I thought I was through with weeping, but stinging tears came again. 'You have suffered so much and for so long. To lose your baby, and to not have your body recover. And then your husband so soon after. Our grief was short-lived but you … twelve years of pain and longing.' I shook my head. 'I cannot even imagine.'

'I suffered more from the high priests and so-called doctors, than from the bleeding.'

I nodded and said, 'You know Jesus told us not to say anything, but how can I not? How can I not share our joy to have our little girl with us again?'

'We are each of us restored. We have been blessed by our Lord's grace.' A twinkle appeared in Rachel's eye, and I knew her words were true. Our friend was indeed herself again. 'You know, He never told me not to say anything.' She glanced at each of us in turn. 'I will tell your story. When I tell mine, I shall tell yours as well.'

We reached for each other's hands and our laughter brought Talitha to the table where she climbed on my lap.

'What is this you have drawn?' I asked.

'While I was sleeping, I had a dream. I saw a beautiful crown.' She presented her drawing to us.

'So many colours. What are they all?'

'They're the gemstones in the crown. I know sapphire, emerald and jasper. Bubbe says that one is ame…ame..'

'Amethyst,' said Deborah.

Talitha nodded and continued pointing to each. 'Onyx, topaz and carnelian.'

'They are the colours of the Lord's grace,' said Rachel. She cast a glance at Deborah then offered her hand. Deborah raised a questioning eyebrow to Jairus as if to ask permission. When he nodded, she took Rachel's hand with both her own.

My heart was full. I squeezed Talitha's waist and thanked God for her life. I smiled at Rachel and thanked Him I could rejoice in her healing too. Jesus had given us both a miracle, His gift of forgiveness and grace.

*Based on* Luke 8:42–56

# Lost at Sea

## M. LESTER DIGHTON

He sat gazing out the window. His face showed the years of hard times, and yet with a care that seemed to frame it all. His hair was fading, but his eyes shone with a fire that seemed to burn deep within. Today, however, there was an expectancy lighting up those eyes even more than usual. His son was coming home! A movement caught his eye, and he saw a car pulling into the drive.

Opening the door, he went out and greeted his son with a big hug that said so much. 'I thought that I had lost you too,' he said. 'Come on in.' He led the way inside. 'Sit down. Do you want anything to eat or drink?'

'No.' A pause. 'Ok.'

They sat down opposite each other. 'Do you want to tell me what happened? They didn't tell me much, and the news just said that you were found alive.' He left it at that.

After a stretch of silence, the words started to flow. 'They're all gone. The skipper, the rest of the deck-hands, my mates—they're just …' A struggle to speak, a choked breath. '… gone!'

The tears trickled down his son's face. 'It was a warm night, and we had finished for the day. Not my turn for watch, and so I just bunked down on the aft-deck to catch some kip. The next thing I knew I was in the water, watching the last of the mast disappear under the waves, and I was swimming. I don't know what or why—it just happened. A float popped up near me, and I swam for it, and just hung on. The water was pleasant, but I felt cold inside. I just remember hanging on to that float, and telling myself not to let go. Well, my arms seemed to freeze around it, and I don't think I could have let go even if I wanted to. I couldn't hear or see anyone else, and only heard the sound of the waves.'

The old man waited, silent, attentive.

'Dad, I drifted for several days, and on the fourth day, I was able to get to this little rock that poked right up out of the ocean. Well, it was more than a little rock, maybe thirty metres high, and a few hundred across. I've got to admit that I prayed to God to save me during that time on the water.' He sat back for a few moments, obviously collecting his thoughts.

Still the old man waited.

'Sure was good to get out of the water. I was starting to attract some fins and they were circling me. Well, that rock was my home for the next forty days. At first, I was just numb inside, but I had to get something to eat. Each day, I would find something to keep me going, but the best part was when I found a small spring coming right out of that rock—unbelievable, in the middle of the ocean, a freshwater spring. It was really good to drink too. The gulls drew it to my attention. As for food, I started out eating a few leaves of this plant each day, some sort of seaweed, and it was alright, but not something I would reach for now I'm home. I tried to look for any eggs near the birds, but it was obviously the wrong time of the year. I remember crying out to God for some meat, and it was then that I remembered the oysters on the rocks along the shoreline. That helped a lot. Occasionally, I'd get to break into a coconut that washed ashore, and the juice was mostly nice, but the flesh wasn't always so good.'

He shifted his gaze to look his father in the eyes. 'Dad, I want to tell you this. While waiting for rescue on that stupid rock sticking out in the middle of the ocean, I thought about God a lot and, funnily enough, many of your stories that you tried to tell me came rushing back. I could have thought about a thousand other things, but NO, it was your silly stories that kept coming back. I went over some of your stories many times. I even started to relate to some of them.' He shook his head.

'Here was a rock saving me in the midst of an ocean of trouble. I even remembered your story about the water coming out of the rock, and it was a water of life. That rock gave me shelter from a couple of storms that came along, and it kept me dry under a bit of an overhang when all else was soaked. It fed me when nothing else could and, I know it's a bit sad to say, but it became something of my friend after a bit.' A smile emerged at last. 'Well, after some forty days, I saw a mast coming near, and so I climbed up to the top of this rock and yelled, and jumped, and waved. Luckily, they saw me, sailed over and picked me up. The rest I think you know. Here I am.'

He settled back into the chair, and tears rolled down his cheeks.

His father finally broke his silence. 'Son, when we heard that your vessel didn't come back to port on time, we started to worry. I was praying to God for your safe return. Well, to be truthful, I always pray for that whenever you are at sea, but this time, I prayed even harder than ever before. Of course I was concerned for you and your safety, but I also know that there is a God in heaven who does hear our prayers, and answers them. So, I always had an inkling that you would be fine, but I still worried as any father would. Our God is faithful, and He answered my prayers. You sitting here now proves that.'

The old man held out a dusty handkerchief as the tears continued to trickle. 'Well, they tried to raise your skipper on the radio, but no good. They went to the radar systems, and your transponder was nowhere to be seen. They contacted other captains in the area to see if anyone had seen or heard from your vessel, but nothing. It was then that they started the search, but they didn't have much to go on as to where to start, except maybe out near the northern banks. That was your boat's last known heading.'

He paused, sighing. 'Son, I just want you to know that I have been praying for you for years, and hoping as well that you would find God like we did—your mother and I, God bless her soul. It seems as if God finally got through to you—not the way I would have chosen, mind you, but I must admit that I am glad that He did.'

He waited, looking for a reaction from his son. Just more tears. 'Ok, so maybe God could have chosen another way to get to you, but He does know what is best.'

A deeper silence followed. His words weren't being pushed away, so he went on. 'While you were talking, I was reminded myself of many of those very same stories I tried to teach you. There was Lazarus, who was in the grave for four days, and Jesus, who is the Rock of Ages, and who called him out of the grave, just like you were called out of the watery grave to the rock. Of course, I do remember telling you about the Rock of Ages on many occasions, and encouraging you to lean on Him when all else fails. I remember the Exodus, where the water came out of the rock, and the forty years in the wilderness. Your forty days is just like their forty years— your time in the wilderness. I remember where I told you He would feed you, and give you drink, and so on for all the other bits that you remembered. However, the story that I am now reminded of the most is the story of the prodigal son, who was lost, and then returned to his father.'

Still no visible reaction.

'Son, you have made me so proud this day. Not just for your safe return to me, but your words about God also fill my heart with joy. Finally, my prayers are being answered. Do you have any idea just how long I have prayed for you to come to God, instead of that lifestyle you were living?' He reached over to clasp his son's hand. 'Welcome home!'

He reached for the young man's shoulder. 'Would you let me pray with you now?'

A simple nod.

He took a deep breath. 'Lord God, we come before You in great thankfulness; let us pray.'

Far-off sounds of rejoicing came faintly to his ears.

*'Our Father, who art in Heaven …'*

# When the Dust Settles

## PAMELA JULIAN

*I'm alive.*

I was standing there in shock. They others had all gone; only Jesus and I remained standing amidst the rubble outside the city. Only He and I knew whether I was guilty; the others didn't. They hated me, wanted to disgrace me. Well, they did that alright.

They dragged me along the streets, half-dressed. In front of everyone! Strangers staring, shocked eyes piercing me. Hate flickering. My best friends saw me; my mother-in-law; my rabbi. They didn't have to do that—they could have left me in a cell, decided the sentence.

I was ashamed, so ashamed. Maybe death was best—I could never again look them in the eye after this.

Caught in the act? If I was guilty, then where was my lover? Why was he not taken for judgment too? I'm not the only one breaking the law here—my accusers are also guilty of that.

*But I'm alive.*

A changed woman certainly, but alive. I could have been a rotting corpse — a feast for the hyenas on unhallowed ground. No burial for a sinner like me. But for that man, Jesus, I would have been.

He's been the talk of the town for a while. He's caused a lot of dissension; some groups are for Him, some against. But He somehow stays out of it; never takes sides. He did it again the other day — that's why I'm alive. It was almost as if the Jewish leaders put Him on trial too — the Romans don't stone for adultery; the Jews do. Was He with the Romans? Or with the Jews? The Pharisees wanted Him to state His side — you could see it. They knew Jewish Law. They asked Him to stand with them and say it: *Stone the adulteress!*

But He didn't. He side-stepped it neatly. Just bent down to the ground and wrote in the dust. Then He stood up and said something to them.

Somehow, His actions conveyed disapproval of the whole lot of them. The righteous ones, the Pharisees, the executors of the law looked just as ashamed as I did — almost as if they, too, had committed a crime deserving a death sentence. I think, if they'd dared, some of them would have killed Him there and then. Instead, they slunk away, the old Rabbi first, then quietly, one by one, leaving just Him, and me.

*So, I'm alive.*

I'm having trouble getting my head around it, but one thing is for sure, I know I've been given a second chance. I feel clean inside—and protected, somehow. I can start afresh—a completely new life. None of them will dare bring this up again, not after that.

I wonder where Jesus is now?

Based on *John 8:1–11*

# The Lady with the Satchel

## TERRY GATFIELD

$\mathcal{I}$ have recently taken to the daily discipline of walking for exercise. The quiet nature reserve greets me most mornings as do our feathered friends. My daily sojourn is lined with the occasional park bench invitation. It was one of those R&R periods that marked this never-to-be forgotten day. Sitting on the bench, by herself, was a very elegant lady, sporting one of the most beautiful leather shoulder satchels I have ever seen. It was of the type you don't buy at Target, K-Mart or on-line. The deep rich dark leather was hand-stitched, and it had a bronze-coloured zip that went from top to bottom. It also sported a number of brass rivets and a stunning tailored clasp. This was the work of an artist.

The lady caught my eye, and I felt embarrassed at being caught staring. She may have thought I was going to mug her and snatch the bag. 'I am sorry, forgive me for being so rude,' I said, 'I could not help noticing how beautiful your satchel is. I have never seen one as finely crafted as that.'

'Thank you.' She smiled. 'I like to think that it is not just a satchel, but it is my world.'

It was delightful she was willing to break the ice and my responses felt less stilted and relaxed.

'Yes,' she said, 'The world is somehow found in my little satchel. It is my personal bank as it is a home for my credit cards. It contains the ticket to my gym and in one of the pockets is a one-dollar coin. This coin rents me a shopping trolley at the supermarket preserving my energy and keeping my walk steady and stable. The same pocket holds a five-dollar note. That pays for my entertainment when I meet a talented busker on my travels. It is my church as it carries a small edition of the Psalms of David. These soothe and enrich my soul. It is my art gallery as it has a picture of my four children, their partners and my wonderful ten grandies. I gaze on them each day and I remember each in prayer.

'The satchel is my hospital as it had to become the custodian of my blood pressure and arrythmia medications. It is my protectorate as it contains a tightly folded plastic poncho in the event of a storm. But above all else it is the touchstone of my son in Tasmania. He lives there with his wonderful wife Rachel and three delightful children. I can't travel there any more due to a lung condition and poor health. I miss him dreadfully. It is he who gave me the satchel. Every day when I leave the house it travels with me. Even more important than that, I sense his spirit travels with me. He is with me now.'

Her soft words concluded and I closed my eyes, the stillness and silence evaporating time. When I opened them she was gone. No lady. No satchel. Just me on the park bench. I was mystified. I looked down and there at my feet was a leather key ring but without any keys. It was wonderfully crafted in a manner similar to the satchel. I held the leather key ring in the palm of my hand firmly, thinking that I needed this reminder to get the keys to unlock so much of my life to set things free. Also to get other keys to lock and safeguard areas that are sacred and special.

I have placed that key ring on a hook by my front door. Every time I leave the house, I carry something of the significance of that key ring just as I carry the mystery of the lady with the satchel.

# Unravelling

## LINDA BARTON

Unravelling the enigma of last night's dream was akin to scratching an itch out of reach. Or a jigsaw missing its guiding image.

Stanley's reverie was abruptly shattered by their golden labrador Jock barking. As he stoked the wood fire alight in the old kitchen, he pulled his coat tight across his chest against the cold. Autumn on the Darling Downs could be frosty. Also the farmhouse, a typical high-set Queenslander with wraparound verandas, promoted ventilation, not insulation. The slow combustion stove would need time to take the chill out of the air.

Stanley filled the cast iron kettle, blackened with age, and placed it on the stove. He enjoyed this time of the day where he could have a moment to himself before he had to answer the demands of running the farm and supporting a family. He thought back to the events of that dark and fateful Sunday six months ago. He shook his head, trying to dislodge the image starting to form. It would take him down a path he did not want to travel. But it was no use. The vision of Ben's lifeless body being dragged from the neighbour's unfenced dam remained indelibly etched in his mind's eye. Blinking, he forced himself to concentrate on the task at hand.

Taking down the tea canister, he measured three teaspoons—one for each person and one for the pot—into the teapot on the table. Beside it he set a china cup and saucer—the one Moo liked. His morning ritual was to make the first pot of tea for the day and take it to Moo, so she could have a sleep-in. It began eight years ago when Ben was born, to spoil the new mother.

Had his own father done the same for his mother? These little rituals sometimes make their way across generations. He knew that sticking to his regular routine was really important now. It provided a concrete tangible structure grounding him and Moo in the present.

He allowed the tea leaves time to steep. In the pause he gathered his thoughts, pondering why the vivid imagery of his dream clawed at his consciousness. Was his fixation a subconscious attempt to distract himself from his own raw sorrow? He placed another lump of wood on the fire. The coals promised to chase away the chill and fill the kitchen with a comforting warmth.

Stanley thought about the many challenges he and Moo had faced together over the past decade. While the flush of first love had faded with the daily rhythm of farm life, he still loved her as much as on their wedding day. In the quiet of the dawn, he whispered a prayer for strength and wisdom. They needed to navigate the stony path of sorrow together and come through, not divided but stronger than ever.

He laid a yellow strawflower he had picked from the field on the tray next to the cup and saucer and, balancing them all, he walked up the narrow hallway. As he paused at the bedroom door, an image from his dream flashed once more before his mind's eye. Should he share it with Muriel? The dream held a complex and mystifying array of scenes of otherworldly beauty, a stark contrast to the sombre reality that gripped them.

Grief had a firm hold on Muriel, his Moo. She took to the refuge of her bed after the accident and daily cried herself to exhaustion. Finally, to sleep. She had taken a sabbatical from life. Stanley felt helpless at her retreat into herself. She'd abandoned her responsibilities as a wife and mother and an active member of their church community. No amount of pleading or prodding from friends, family or their minister could persuade her to accept the loss and incorporate it into a new existence. Perhaps sharing his subconscious wanderings could provide a momentary escape, a connection, a shared experience to ease the burden of sorrow that lay so heavy between them. Stanley hesitated, wary that such a revelation might seem trivial, given their profound loss. His heart sank with the weight of the decision, sizing up the delicate balance between connection and isolation, hope and insensitivity. The air was already thick with her unspoken words and his unshed tears. A choice awaited him. Would sharing his dream be a bridge or a barrier?

Stanley fixed a smile to his face as he offered Muriel a warm 'Good morning.'

She buried her face and pulled the covers higher. He placed the tray on the nightstand, then drew back the curtains and opened the window. Crisp morning air and the cheerful chirping of birds filled the room. It was crucial for Muriel to confront their altered circumstances. There was a farm that demanded their joint efforts; little Anne to nurture at the vulnerable age of five, a darling girl who required the love and guidance of both parents. Stanley felt he could not battle on as a solo parent much longer.

Dewdrops sparkled in the sunlight on the leaves outside the window. They reminded Stanley of an image from his dream—a many-faceted diamond. In that instant, his earlier reservations dissolved. Perhaps, disclosing the dream could be the key to unlocking their hearts. It might allow them to embrace a new future without Ben. He recalled the minister's sermon last Sunday. It highlighted dreams as a conduit for divine communication and pointed out the many pivotal biblical events that began during sleep. Stanley felt reassured his dream was important. With newfound resolve, he turned towards the bed, ready to unveil his cryptic vision to Muriel.

The room was silent except for the soft rustling of the doona as Stanley settled himself on the edge of the bed. The strawflower, a symbol of undying love and remembrance, spun slowly between his fingers, its papery petals brushing against his skin. He closed his eyes, taking a deep breath, seeking the tranquillity to disentangle the jumbled thoughts in his mind. With a quiet invocation to the Holy Spirit, he sought not just the right words, but the empathy and insight to mend what was broken, to soothe the unseen wounds with a balm made of hope and understanding.

As his eyes lingered on the pale walls, images of past joy danced in the air around him. He recalled the dream's tapestry, each thread a vivid image woven from the depths of his subconscious. The narrative was not linear like a film with its acts clearly defined; rather, it was a kaleidoscope of moments, each shifting into the next. Singular images would emerge, stark and arresting, only to be swallowed by scenes of bewildering complexity. The dream's essence was elusive, a mosaic of fragmented beauty and enigma, challenging him to decipher its meaning.

He begins to speak.

Stanley describes the initial vision that crystallised in his consciousness: a diamond, a traditional emblem of loyalty, purity, and love-laden bonds. His thoughts drift to Ben, a rare and precious gift, who had infused their lives with immense happiness. He tells of the diamond shifting into a monolith as vast as Uluru. According to Aboriginal ancestral lore, the rock emerged from the earth's sorrow over a devastating conflict that claimed the lives of leaders from two warring tribes. Stanley reveals his own sorrow, suppressed for half a year, is just as monumental as Uluru and can no longer be contained.

He wipes away the tears flowing down his face with the back of his hand. He hears Muriel struggling to muffle her own sorrow.

He hesitates, then describes the next scene in the sequence. A dragon is lying in a sunlit glade, his head pillowed on a reed bed by the banks of a gentle stream. It seems so fantastical, Stanley is almost too embarrassed to continue. Yet he presses on, captivated by the image of the dragon with a teardrop trickling down its cheek, radiating bright iridescent blues and greens that echo the hues on its dorsal scales. The scene is both touching and sorrowful. With a jolt, Stanley recalls the dragon symbolises Ben's birth year in Chinese tradition. He remembers that according to mythology, dragon tears have unparalleled healing powers. Surely this is a sign. Muriel has wept a thousand tears or more since Ben's death.

Stanley detects a shift in the air, as Muriel moves closer to him. He suppresses the impulse to reach out and comfort her. He focuses on the unfolding story captured in his dream.

It's a liminal space—half-dreaming, half-awake. He reaches out with his left hand, a gesture that echoes the image in his mind. Beneath his palm, he senses a soft rain falling upon the stream, creating ripples that spread towards the bank where the dragon sleeps peacefully. Muriel stirs, propping herself up next to Stanley with a pillow supporting her head. Hesitant to continue, Stanley looks to her for reassurance.

Nodding, she whispers, 'Rain heralds rebirth, and water is the giver of life.' Taking her words as a cue, Stanley closes his eyes to enhance his recall. Moments later, he extends his left hand, then his right. 'My right hand cradles a small blue duck egg, smooth as a pebble,' he explains.

Muriel places her hand gently on Stanley's shoulder and murmurs, 'I'm wondering about the significance of these images. Perhaps the first reaching hand symbolises your humanity and the struggle to hold on to Ben? Are we clinging on to him and holding him back? Perhaps it means that we, not just you, should let him go. If that's the case, then the other reaching hand might signify Jesus, and Ben's redemption.'

Stanley is taken aback by Muriel's sudden change. She has been unresponsive and disengaged for so long her words render him speechless. Muriel muses, 'For millennia across the world, the egg has been a powerful symbol representing the earth, fertility and resurrection.' Muriel's grip tightens on his shoulder and she nudges him. 'So,' she prompts, 'What do you think?'

Stanley strokes his chin. He silently expresses gratitude to the Holy Spirit for the courage and the means to dissolve the ominous quiet that had settled between him and Muriel since Ben's passing.

Now with a starting point, healing seems possible.

'What if I document the dream and ask the minister's perspective during his coming visit?'

Muriel leans into him, and murmurs her approval. Then, with a touch of timidity, she requests, 'Would you please reheat the tea? And the day is moving on; little Annie will stir soon and want her breakfast.' She pauses, then throws off the doona. 'I'll just get up and make it for her.'

## Scripture

As the Scriptures tell us that dreams are one of the most common ways God speaks (Numbers 12:6), that they are made accessible to us through the gift of the Holy Spirit (Acts 2:16–17) and that many of the great biblical events began while someone was sleeping (e.g. Genesis 15:8–21.)

The dream sequence and interpretation is based on an entry from my own journal following the death of my son.

# In Jesus' Footsteps

## JO WANMER

'*I* wonder if she is OK?'
It was a passing thought, that slivered into my unguarded
  heart.
I drove on.

But what if she isn't? I slam the door on my soft heart.
She looked pregnant, sitting in the gutter.
But what sort of girl sits in the gutter by a main road?
She could be a prostitute, or on drugs or… I shuddered and
pushed down my thoughts.
But what if she is sick, or in labour, or homeless?
I thought of my granddaughters. So often they needed help,
a lift, a hug, an encouraging word.
Well… even if she is homeless, it's her problem.
I swiped away a tear, and swallow the next ones.
It's none of my business.

Why then have I turned off?
It could be life has dealt her a raw deal?
Maybe she's been evicted.
Whatever will happen to that innocent baby? I can't ignore
    a baby.
But it's not my problem

Well, whose problem is it?
It's hers.
My car slowed to turn back onto the main road, staying in
    the left lane.
I'm not stopping. I'll just check…
But I think she's crying.
Keep going… not my business

My car stops.
My arms are around her.
Her face is on my shoulder.
Her dirty hair sends repugnant odours up my nose.
I pull her away from the road.
Horns blast my car because it's in a no-stopping zone.
There is only one thing to do.
I shove her in the front seat.
She points to a bag under the bus stop, but no words are
    spoken.
As I drive away, a warm peace floods over me and through
    the car.

She relaxes. 'Jesus… You came.'

# Flesh and Stone

## REBEKAH ROBINSON

The sky was pearling with dawn as Jesus entered the Temple precinct for the day's teaching, lowering Himself to sit down. A good day to birth a lesson. He wondered what He would see the Father do today and lifted His heart in habitual surrender. People were gathering already, about their tasks and curiosities, while the cool held.

Shouldering to the front of the group came the usual suspects: two pugnacious-looking Pharisees, today with a gleam in their eyes and a grip on a girl. Jesus gave an inward sigh. *I'll need all Your wisdom with this one, Spirit.*

The men thrust the woman towards Jesus. Bareheaded and scantily clad, hair askew, she made a futile grab for as much fabric to cover herself as she could. This was difficult with pinioned arms. She looked for all the world like she'd been dragged from her bed. Or someone else's. She did not look up, but her face flamed. The crowd murmured and jostled. A titter broke out.

'Filthy adulteress,' one of her accosters spat. 'We caught this whore in the very act of adultery.'

*In the act?* Jesus said nothing at first. *So... you were there, then? Interesting.*

He barely glanced at the woman, but craned His neck ostentatiously and peered out over the crowd, His expressive brows arched. Realising He was scanning for the woman's partner in crime, the Pharisees hemmed and hawed a little, and closed ranks.

*So... I wonder if it was one of you, then. Or, at the very least, if you set a trap for this poor woman for reasons of your own, while you were setting a trap for Me. Is she nothing more to her shepherds than collateral damage? We have strayed far, haven't we? You 'love' God with your mind and strength, but not your heart and soul. And as for your neighbour...*

The Pharisees were having none of His reputed egalitarian poppycock. 'In the Law, Moses commanded us to stone such women. What do you say?'

*Well, first of all, I say, 'that's a misquote, Mr. Expert-in-the-Law.' Moses said to stone both parties. And second of all, very clever. If I say, 'Yes, let's stone her,' the Romans will be all over Me like tiles on a terrace. And if I say, 'No,' you'll denounce Me as unMosaic.*

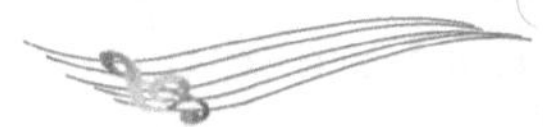

The woman cringed. It would have to be Rabbi Yeshua, wouldn't it? The man she had watched wistfully from afar, the holiest man in town, the compassionate one. Rumour had it he was willing to touch lepers, bypass angels, and feed the hungry. She had seen other working girls around him. If He was willing to talk to *them*... oh, but the whole thing was impossible. He was a man; he would never understand her situation. He was good; he would never condone her sin. He wasn't a Levitical priest, so he couldn't even absolve her over a sacrifice, not even if he wanted to. Never mind the small voice of hope, babbling in the back of her head. However different he was, he was still a rabbi. The Law was his life. And now she couldn't even look at him. Tears began to leak out. She could die today. She could *die*. She whimpered. *Be hard,* she admonished herself. *They will be.*

The crowd waited breathlessly to see what would happen next. The fate of the woman was obvious: she was going to get what she deserved. It remained to be seen, however, how the strange young rabbi would handle this. *Mr. Upright,* they called him. No one had ever seen him flout the Law, yet he carried himself with a freedom and unselfconscious ease normally reserved for insolent rebels. His attitudes were... curious. His speeches were obscure, at least on the surface, though they had a way of cutting through to the heart. No one doubted his fervour for God or his knowledge of the Law; he was famous for that, if a little unorthodox in its application. It was his confident assertions and scandalous declarations—

not to mention his weird attitude to the lowest of people—that had everyone baffled. What would he do? Take one look at those long, slim legs and find her later? He wouldn't be the first to follow up such a lead. Tell everyone she was 'just misunderstood'? Or go the other way—declaim her sin with a lofty speech about purity? Or a completely unrelated story? Would the Pharisees finally get something they could pin on him? Everyone waited for whatever outrageous thing Jesus was going to say next.

And he continued to say nothing.

*The Law of Moses came from You, Father,* Jesus prayed inwardly. *It is Your Holy Word. You gave it to Moses after We led this people out of Egypt. I engraved it on stone with My own finger. Commandments, promises and warnings. I remember writing on stone in the last days of Babylon, too. I wrote of judgment, that time.* He rubbed his finger and thumb together absently, brow furrowed.

And then into His mind from the Father came the vivid memory of a much earlier scene. A primeval garden. Colour and beauty. The dust of the earth, formed into a living being. The excitement of the bestowing of breath and name and spirit and destiny, the wonder at watching it quicken. Jesus caught His own breath; He knew what to do. He bent over slowly, and as He did, so did everyone else. Suspense swelled. Stones trembled in anticipation.

Jesus extended a finger and began to write in the dust. Every eye was on that writing finger; none were on the woman. *I can write her a new identity*, He thought. *It is the right of God to create life from dirt, beauty from ashes, art from atoms. It is a higher and earlier law. And it is a good deal more flexible than stone. 'Can I not do with you, Israel, as this potter does?' We said to Jeremiah. 'Like clay in the hand of the potter, so are you in My hand, Israel.'*

The moment stretched.

'Well,' broke in the other Pharisee, 'don't just sit there. Tell us what you think! Don't you take sin seriously, young man? What's Moses worth, then? Is all this "perfectly all right" with you? Oh, let's *all* forsake the Law and do exactly as we please! In fact, let's throw in some *pregnancy*, shall we?' He leered, suddenly personal.

Other voices chimed in. Jesus let them build and train their focus on him. The woman watched Him writing, and He heard her take a few shallow breaths of respite.

When the psychological moment arrived, when they had dug themselves in good and proper, He straightened up, shading His eyes with one hand against the morning sun. With little inflection, He spoke mildly into the sudden lull. 'Let any one of you who is without sin be the first to throw a stone at her.'

And you could have heard a pin drop. They had all forgotten that He was descended from the family of Solomon. None of them knew He had *created* Solomon.

Jesus leaned over again and continued to write on the ground. He did not look around.

One by one, the crowd began to dissipate. The elders went first. They knew their long history of inability to avoid sin—some with self-awareness, others with simple hard experience. The throng dwindled as even the youngest and most brash saw their culpability. Hadn't He said that just *lusting* after a woman was heart-adultery? Could you stone your own heart? There was only one person present who was without sin. In a singularly courteous gesture, Jesus kept His eyes on the ground, declining to ogle man's walk of shame.

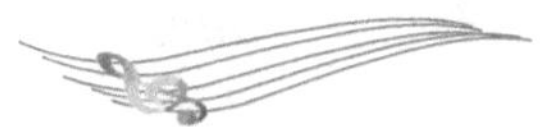

The woman massaged the feeling back into her upper arms, marvelling at how quickly even the most arrogant of her accusers had realised their mistake, and marvelling more at the strange man before her showing gentleness rather than staring down the vanquished. She eyed him cautiously. Before her, unbending now, sat the only person who was qualified to throw a stone of judgment. His heart, it was clear, was neither judgmental nor stone-like.

And she did not need a heart of stone either. She wanted a heart of flesh. An overheard phrase floated up from her memory: *'And I will put My Spirit within you and cause you to walk in My statutes.'* Ezekiel? And another: *'I will put My law in their minds and write it on their hearts. I will be their God, and they will be My people.'* Jeremiah. Was that really possible, after all? For *her*?

'Where did they all go?' the rabbi asked, looking about in mock surprise. *Was that sarcasm?* 'Has no one condemned you?'

He was looking directly into her eyes, *oh Lord God help me.* 'No one, sir,' she choked out. There was only him. She waited for the blow to fall.

'Then neither do I condemn you,' Jesus declared. His kind eyes reflected the sun like a candle flame into hers. She couldn't look away. 'Go now... and leave your life of sin.'

Her heart beat, twice—flesh indeed—and she blinked. Her mouth was dry. *He can't mean it. Can he? I am... free? Lord God...*

# Captivated

## PAMELA JULIAN

Summer night—Antarctica
Twilight smooths the razored rocks
sharp white slurs to softer grey
sapphire waters slide to neutral hue
and that endless swathe of perfect blue
slips into deeper shades unnamed; so too

the jagged edges of my discontent
that red-raw pain, and glittering ice
of helpless rage blanches to beige—
as in reverence I gaze

Soaring rocks display Your might;
pristine icebergs, untouched snow
Your Holiness, like this far Pole
unfamiliar and unknown—
only those who truly seek You
dare to venture, deep
into Your wild and untamed heart

And none of earth's defilements touch
Your breath, Your living water—
they sluice away my petty pasts,
detach me from the snares
that trapped me,
in the hopes and hurts of life.

Your splendour entrances my soul.
Lost in You, I'm freed,
enthralled
I risk my all
to journey into You

(First Prize
– Trinity College Queensland
*Faith and the Arts Competition 2022*)

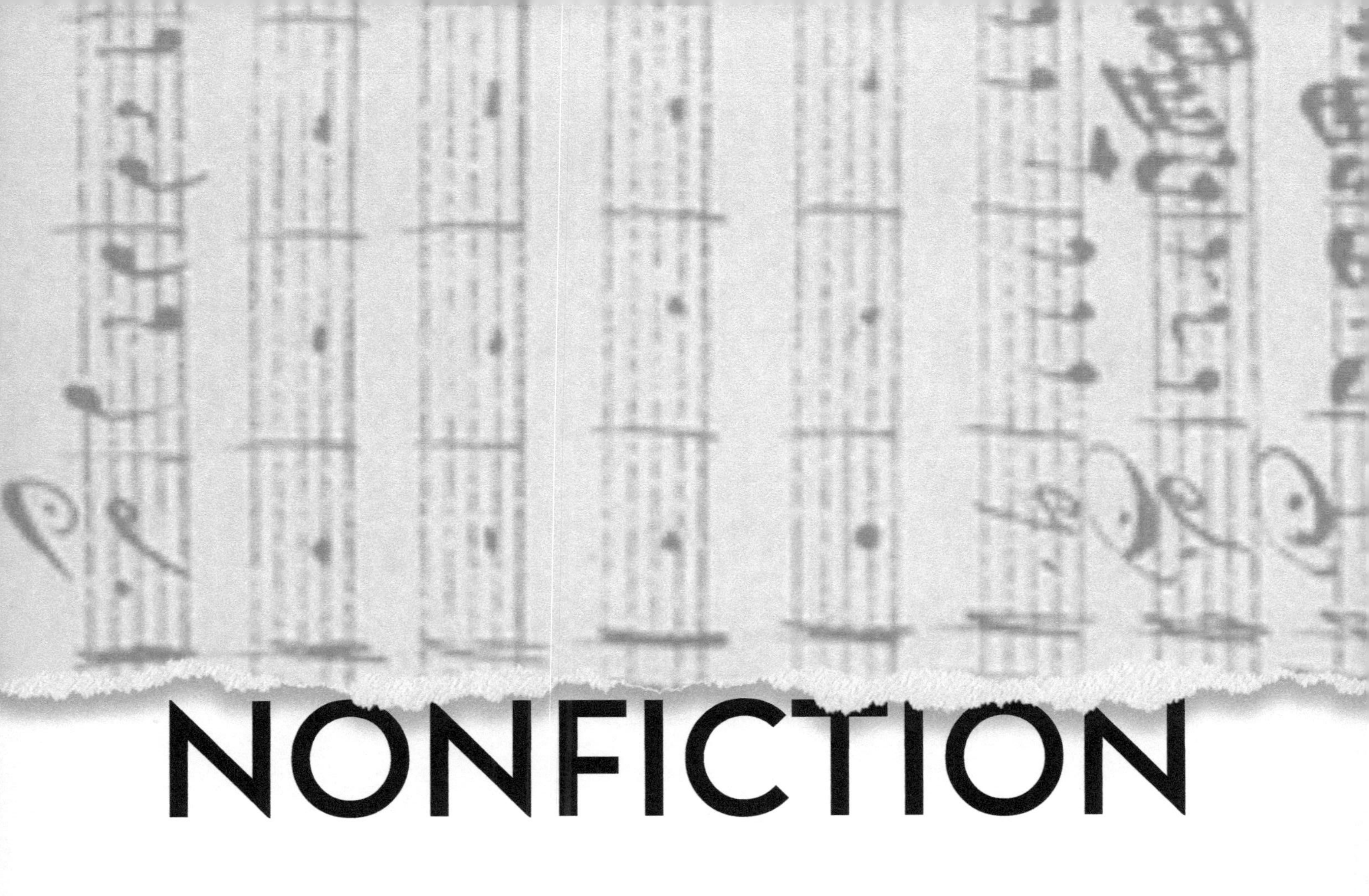

NONFICTION

# Never Early, Never Late

## SANDRA FLORENTINA

*I*n 1999 the most incredible God-event happened. After years of crippling pain and menstrual flooding from endometriosis, life was unbearable. My gynaecologist recommended a hysterectomy, and I was booked in for the operation. All seemed well, but little did I know that God had a much greater plan in mind.

One week before the surgery, I felt the Lord laid these words on my heart while praying: 'Daughter, there will be complications but do not fear for I will show you that I have all of this under My control. Remember this, three nurses who you don't know will come from various parts of the hospital and I will place My words into their mouths. They will say "You don't know me, but I am a Christian and I'm here to tell you that God has it."'

After the surgery, I had serious complications due to a pre-existing bleeding disorder. I bled internally and felt like my body was on fire. I almost died and was put in the ICU where they had to give me three bags of blood. I also had a large blood clot in my pelvis. It felt like someone was using a blowtorch inside me, and the doctors couldn't get the pain under control. In my head I was screaming, 'Father, I'm in trouble. Help me. You are all that I have left. No one truly knows the pain I am feeling.'

He answered my prayer, and I felt His peace that surpasses understanding descend on me like a shower of rain on parched land. But the pain got worse again. I couldn't cope, so I fell in and out of consciousness. The pain kept trying to drag me away from God, but I knew I had to stand firm. It was like being physically choked and I could hardly take a breath. When I thought I couldn't do this pain anymore, I again screamed in my head, 'Father help me or take me home.'

Then the first nurse came from another part of the hospital into the ICU. She whispered in my ear, 'You don't know me, but I am here to tell you that God's got it.' Those words were so comforting—but the tug-of-war with pain resurfaced and this time I wanted the Lord to take me home. I felt like I was only able to hold onto God by a thread.

Two agonising days later, whilst still in intensive care, another nurse came and said, 'You don't know me, but I am here to tell you that God's got it.' I was in a mess because the constant pain was like a jagged knife that kept being pushed into my body, tearing it apart. After the nurse's word, I cried for help to the Lord. This was all that I could hang onto, remembering the suffering that Jesus went through. As I focussed on Christ again, I felt His peace wash over me as if He had wrapped His soft blanket of grace around me to comfort me.

Still very unwell, I developed a significant arrhythmia. My heart felt like it was banging out of my ribcage, and I couldn't get away from the thumping and banging noise of my heartbeat in my eardrums. It was also hard to breathe. I felt I couldn't get enough air into my lungs and that led to panic attacks. I couldn't escape the iron grip of fear. In desperation I asked, 'Lord, why is this happening? I'm broken. How much more pain do I need to bear for Your glory? I feel like I am drowning in quicksand.'

The more I struggled, the worse it got. The quicksand took hold of my broken body and was trying to pull me under. When the mire seemed to be up to my neck strangling me, I was defeated and gave up. I cried out, 'Lord, do what You want with me for I am too weak to do anything.'

But the Lord brought back to mind that the third nurse hadn't come. This terrified me even more because I still didn't know God's plans for this suffering and what I'd experienced to date had been horrendous. 'Do I now have to suffer with a heart attack as well for Your glory? When will this journey end, Father?'

I had so many questions which were not answered, and I couldn't see how all of this would bring Him glory. It was like going down rapids without an oar whilst being smashed into the rocks at every turn. I finished pleading for God to help me. Then the third nurse came and said, 'You don't know me, but I am here to tell you that God's got it.'

I tried to hold onto His peace but at that point it kept slipping through my hands as if I was trying to grab water. This led to even greater anguish—I should be able to do this, but I can't. This despair was like an anaconda squeezing the life out of me.

The next day, my doctors told me they were sending me to the cardiac ward in a Brisbane hospital, two hours away, where they could monitor my arrhythmias. My three daughters, aged 9 to 16, visited me. Their long pale faces dripping tears pierced my heart. They needed their mother. I felt even more useless than a worn-out dishrag.

I was terrified about going to Brisbane, with so many negative thoughts I felt my head was going to explode. My logical brain was out for the count, so all I knew to do was to pray that God would reveal what He wanted me to see or do in Brisbane. How did I know about this? It's because God has always used my health problems for His glory. There have been countless times in my life when all I could do was to hold His hand like a child as He walked with me in the journey of suffering. When I fell down under the pressure, He carried me through each traumatic event. His embrace was loving, warm and gentle. His grace was like a lifeline, as a baby in the womb depends on their mother's umbilical cord to survive.

He again used a broken claypot like me to implement His will in the most amazing way. I arrived at the hospital by ambulance late in the afternoon. The next day, God placed on my heart that I needed to speak to the woman in the next room. I knocked and went in and saw a little old lady whose face was full of anger and anguish. She looked at me angrily and snapped, 'You're a Christian, aren't you?'

I saw how upset she was and spoke quietly. 'Yes, I am a Christian.'

'Well, I prayed this morning for God to show Me that He is real and I need to tell you how angry I am with Him.'

My heart went out to her. 'What happened?'

'When I was teenager I wore red lipstick, and I was told I was going to hell which destroyed me. Another time, I went to the movies and held a boy's hand, and I was told I was a sinner.'

'That's spiritual abuse,' I replied. 'It's not from God because He is not concerned about whether you wear lipstick or not. He cares about your heart.'

Her eyes filled with tears, and she wept for what seemed like a very long time. Then she released the distress she had carried for seventy years in a guttural scream. It shocked me and sent a shiver up my spine. I sat with her for hours, continually encouraging her that her Saviour was ready and willing to wrap her in His blanket of grace.

I asked if I could hug her, and she said yes. She never wanted to let me go. I felt so much compassion for her. The more I spoke about God's love, the more the anger and anguish etched in her face faded away. She looked at me and said, 'I believe in Him. Thank you very much.'

I was overjoyed. 'Welcome, sister in Christ, to God's family'.

'I have waited my whole life to hear those words.' Then the most glorious smile appeared on her face, and it was as if she had been able to let go of all the abuse she had suffered.

She told me she was tired, so I got up to leave. 'I'll come back in the morning to see how you are.'

She held her arms out and motioned for me to come over. She wrapped her arms around me again. 'I now have something to look forward to when God takes me home.'

I agreed and left her room saying again, 'I'll be back,' and she said, 'I know.'

The next morning, her bed was empty. When I asked the nurse where the little old lady was, she said, 'I cannot give you any details, but she died this morning.'

This is when I knew that God had used the complications from my surgery for His glory. I felt humbled by this whole experience, but sad that I wouldn't see her again. All she needed was unconditional love. I was astonished because it was in His perfect timing that I spoke to her. He's never early, never late. He placed me where He wanted me to be to touch this lady's heart. I knew for sure that God had brought me to Brisbane for His purpose of showing her His incredible love before calling her to be with Him.

But there remains the burning question of whether I am angry with God for allowing me to go through so much suffering for His purposes. I can honestly say that, if He wanted to use me again for His glory, then of course I would go through whatever He wanted because I want to serve Him every day of my life. My walk with the Lord isn't easy, but I wouldn't want to change it ever. Being open to suffering for God's glory is an incredible honour, but it is not to be taken lightly. Once we truly understand God's sovereignty over everything that happens, whether it be good or bad, then it changes our focus from ourselves to God.

I couldn't stop crying while writing this piece because it's now 2024 and I have Multiple Sclerosis which affects my swallowing, my stomach, my bowel, my bladder and my kidneys. I have constant pain, vertigo and nausea. I feel like I'm walking in jelly, and if a pavement is uneven, then I feel completely unsteady and incredible nausea sets in. I have problems with thermoregulation because I have lesions in my brain stem. My temperature moves between hypothermia — very low body temperature — to feeling my body is on fire and being crippled by ambient temperatures above 25°C (77°F). I have another disease, Erythromelalgia, 'burning feet syndrome', and when it is flaring my feet look like they have been boiled in oil and I must anaesthetise them with a ketamine compound so I can walk. This syndrome has now spread to my ears which I have to anaesthetise as well. I have another autoimmune disease, Raynaud's disease, that leads to a lack of blood supply to my hands in cold weather, so I must anaesthetise them too in order to control the pain.

Progression of these autoimmune diseases will eventually lead to my death, so I am in the same boat again that I was in 1999. Hence the tears.

As hard as it is, deep down I wouldn't change a thing. All my trauma has led to a deeper walk with God, and has been used to encourage others. True comfort can only be achieved by being held in the arms of Jesus. Until He calls me home, I live to serve Him.

# New Sight

## DELL SADDLER HAMILTON

*'This happened so that the works of God*
*would be displayed…*
*While I am in the world, I am the Light of the World.'*

*John* 9:3–5 BSB

John and Joan* were a married couple who had come to Queensland from an interstate mining town to participate in a healing course. My husband and I ministered to them as they worked through the blockages to effective prayer in their lives. Joan was colour-blind and had only ever seen the world in shards of grey. During the last session of the last day she received prayer for healing.

They had decided to have a short break in the Sunshine Coast hinterland before returning home. A few hours after the prayer, they were driving along the main road from our hometown of Maleny along the ridge to Montville. Joan was gazing out the passenger window, observing the rolling hills

*Not their real names.

and deep valleys, when she started to scream hysterically.

Shocked, her husband pulled over and stopped the car.

'Look at that! Look at that!' Joan shrieked.

'Look at what?' John asked, puzzled.

They had stopped at a dip in Balmoral Road that overlooks Lake Baroon. The sun was just setting in the west and was reflected on the water when Joan saw in colour for the very first time in her life—a brilliant gold sunset over a peaceful blue lake surrounded by green mountains. God switched on her sight to gem-fire beauty in one splendid moment.

But this is not all there is to this story.

John had been part of a prayer ministry group that I had led. At one point I asked him to answer immediately and without thinking the following question: 'When you think of your hometown, what colours do you see?'

He answered immediately, 'Various shades of grey.' I asked him where else he had a home during his life but he had always lived in this mining town. The world around him had, as far back as he could remember, been dull, dingy and dreary. His spirit had absorbed the drabness of the town and its surrounding area.

There were two miracles that happened that day. Two people were set free to live a life filled with vibrant colour. One was healed spiritually and the other was healed physically.

Lake Baroon from the road to Montville

# The Dark and the Light

## PAMELA JULIAN

He sipped his drink. Fifty, if he was a day. Occasionally his eyes strayed towards her—young, pretty, foreign. She didn't meet his look. They didn't talk; just sat and sipped. I could see her thoughts of *Here we go again*—resignation in her eyes at the night ahead.

Other girls stood and sat around. Their eyes reflected hopelessness and despair. Except for one teenager—her eyes were pits of fear.

Further down the road, a group of girls in green bikinis swayed to music. How many were eighteen? Another group in white bikinis giggled and flirted each time a man passed by.

After walking through the city's red-light district, our tour group was subdued. I thought of those young girls doing this night after night, and my heart ached. I regarded the men who used them with disgust and anger. Trafficking is appalling.

Later that night, when debriefing with our team leader, he said, 'Pray for the men, too. They are just as lost and empty as the girls.' I realised the truth of what he said: any man looking to give meaning to his life by a brief encounter with a foreign teenager has truly lost his way. And not only his own way, what does he model to other men? To his work colleagues? To his son?

Our trip to Asia included sightseeing in major cities. We simply do not have cities this size in Australia—the visibility of the poverty was a shock. People here earn what they can in any way they can, and some have been caught in prostitution rings. On another street, a shrivelled old lady was sitting, begging, on a cloth on the pavement. Then I saw two toddlers with her—and she lifted the baby to her breast. I gasped. I realised she was probably in her twenties—exhausted from a lifetime of 'night-work'.

Children and teens who have been rescued now live in homes, improving their literacy, and learning some English. They are learning new ways to live, and ways to earn money respectably, to support their families. Part of their rescue program included attending church, so we went with them. And the glow on their faces! We rejoiced at their smiles, their pleasure in worship, and the spark in their eyes. They radiated the new life Jesus gives.

I could not help but compare the eyes of anguish with the joyous eyes of those who were discovering the healing that Jesus brings. I started to see the power of transformation that God works in people's lives.

# Muffy the Matchmaker
## NOLA LORRAINE

'And please, Lord, can I have a dog and a husband. Amen.'

My husband thinks it's funny that I put the dog first, but it's lucky I did. That dog was instrumental in choosing the husband.

I always imagined I'd be married in my twenties. By the time thirty-five rolled around and there were no knights in shining armour beating a path to my door, I started to wonder if I'd missed the boat (or the jousting tournament or wherever it is knights hang out these days). Some of my single friends were diligently praying for the man of their dreams, even asking for long lists of qualities that person should have. I only had two things on my list—he had to love God above everything else and he had to be a good communicator. I figured everything else would fall into place if those two things were taken care of first.

I wasn't just desperate and dateless. I desperately wanted a dog. I'd owned a cocker spaniel during my high school and uni years, but had since lived in rental accommodation where I couldn't have pets. I thought that was about to change when I moved into a house owned by some friends of mine. They said I could have a dog as soon as they got the backyard fenced. After months passed, then a year, then a few more months, I was wondering if they'd just given lip service to the fence. Would I ever be able to get that dog?

I was in Tasmania on summer holidays when I said the 'dog and husband' prayer. The friend I was visiting had to work that day, so I decided to fast and pray for the coming year. I prayed about my work situation, family and friends, newfound relatives, ministry activities, future directions, and possibly even world peace and my own syndicated television show. It was almost as an afterthought that I tacked the dog and husband before the 'Amen', but God was listening.

Within days of arriving home, my landlady told me they'd lined up a tradie to install the fence. I went out that weekend, bought a stack of dog food and accessories, and announced to my friends that I was getting a dog called Muffy.

'What sort is she?' they asked.

'I don't know,' I said. 'I haven't bought her yet.'

The fence did indeed go up the next week, so I looked in the Saturday newspaper to see which dogs were on sale. I wanted something small and fluffy and thought the Pomeranian puppy would fit the bill. I drove to the designated address, the seller handed me the dog, she licked my nose (the dog, not the seller), and it was love at first sight. I'd found my Muffy. Answer to prayer? Tick!

When Muffy was still only a few months old, I started dating a fellow I'd met line dancing at a Christian singles mixer. The fact that I could count and turn on cue automatically made me one of the best dancers in the room, so it was a *fait accompli* that 'Dave' would ask me out. Woo hoo! God must be answering my prayer request for a husband as well. Then miracle of miracles, Tim from our Christian staff group rang and asked if I'd like to go out for a coffee.

'Oh, that would be really nice,' I said, 'but I'm actually going out with someone.' A brainwave percolated. 'I'm having a few friends around tomorrow to meet Dave. Would you like to come?'

Poor Tim. I had no idea that he was keen on me, but he agreed to pop round to meet the new boyfriend. Muffy, being the party animal that she was, greeted him with gusto. He looked down at her and said, 'You must be Muffy.' She was smitten, but I already had a man in my life.

Dave came to my house a few times and seemed to like Muffy, even suggesting we take her with us on a picnic one day. However, his true colours came out when visiting my parents. Pomeranians are very effervescent little critters, so while Dave was talking to my mother, Muffy jumped up and down on his leg trying to get his attention. Dave completely ignored her. He didn't even hold his hand out to her. To be fair, he may have been nervous meeting my parents and was trying to make a good impression on them, but they weren't the only ones he had to impress.

'You didn't greet Muffy,' I said later.

He looked at me blankly. 'I didn't greet Muffy?'

We went on a few more dates, but the writing was on the wall. The next time he came to my house, Muffy barked at him. The fluffball had spoken.

I waited a month or so before telling Tim I'd broken up with Dave, and we started going out soon after. The next time Tim came over, Muffy jumped onto his lap and fell asleep. It was a good sign.

Then Tim surprised me by popping the question after just a few months of dating. Yes, *that* question. I answered the way any romantically-inclined woman would: 'Are you out of your mind?'

Okay, not my shiniest moment and I wish I could jump in the TARDIS and go back in time to redo my answer. But what I really meant was that it was too soon in our relationship to ask that question. I was notoriously bad at making life-changing decisions and this was definitely one I wanted to be sure about. I couldn't think of anything worse than saying, 'Yes,' and then backing out. To my way of thinking, I was sparing Tim from my indecisiveness. I don't think Tim saw it quite the same way, though he did seem to accept my request to wait six months before asking the question again.

In the meantime, he racked up more brownie points when he looked after Muffy one night. He set up her little doggy loafer next to his bed, where she happily slept until about midnight. Then a huge clap of thunder reverberated through the room. Muffy hurled herself onto Tim's hairy chest and clung there for the duration of the storm. It was a hot, steamy summer's night—not the best time to have a furry Pomeranian sprawled across your body like a little hot water bottle, but it was ten out of ten for a bonding experience.

Even though Muffy had chosen who she wanted for her Dad, I still wrestled with it. I loved Tim and he met the lofty criteria I'd set—he loved God more than anything else and he was a good communicator. He was also kind-hearted and we had a lot of things in common, but I was afraid of making a mistake. I'd thought Dave was 'the one' and then a few red flags made me realise he wasn't. Now I thought Tim was 'the one', but what if he wasn't?

I went away by myself for a weekend to do some serious thinking. While I was praying, God gave me a beautiful picture of Tim and I doing a skating routine. I love watching the pairs competitions where the skaters are in perfect sync with each other. There's one particularly beautiful move in which the man effortlessly hoists the woman up above his head so that her body is horizontally balanced on one of his hands while he whizzes around the ice. That was the image God gave me, even though my only foray into figure-skating consisted of a few feeble attempts during the Torvill and Dean era. I got to the stage where I could slowly move forward without falling over and then decided to quit while I was ahead. Tim has a disability, which meant he used a walking stick in those days, so skating wasn't even a possibility. Yet there we were in my mind, skating in perfect unison. It had to be a spiritual metaphor or a glimpse of heaven. I had my answer.

Still, I'm a bit slow on the uptake. Rather than telling Tim as soon as I got back, I waited another couple of days. I had to be extra sure. In the absence of a spare fleece to toss on the lawn, à la Gideon, I took myself off for an early-morning swim to clear my head. It was a small pool at a local gym and there was only one other person there—a grey-haired older man I'd never seen before. The only problem was that this grey-haired gent was a very sociable chatty type. Every time I came up for air, he asked me a question. How was I ever going to think straight with him trying to start up a conversation? If only I could tumble-turn like Shane Gould, I wouldn't have to answer him, but he was too quick for me.

'Where do you work?'

'At the uni,' I said and ducked my head under the water for the next lap.

On the return leg, he tried again. 'You don't know Tim Passmore, do you?'

It turns out they went to church together. There were hundreds of employees at my uni, yet God sent one of Tim's friends to a random pool at that moment to help me tick my final box. Okay God, I think you're trying to tell me something!

Later that day, I told Tim that I loved him and would marry him. It hadn't occurred to me that he might have changed his mind in the interim. He hadn't. Phew!

He looked visibly relieved. 'That was a long time to wait.'

'But I was early,' I said.

He did a double-take. 'How do you work that out?'

'I told you to ask me again in six months, but I only took five. I'm early.'

On our wedding day, my housemate brought Muffy to the venue where we were having the official photos taken and put her at my feet.

'Will she just sit there?' the photographer asked.

'No, I'll pick her up,' I said. I held her between us, the photographer snapped some pics, and we got on with the rest of the day, including an alarming burst of the Macarena at the reception. It wasn't until we saw the photos several weeks later that we realised the significance of that moment. Muffy is looking straight at the camera with a huge smile across her face, and her right paw is reaching out and touching Tim on the shoulder. It was as if she was saying, 'This is my daddy.'

Tim and I have been happily married for twenty-six years and he truly is my soulmate. Muffy was with us for more than fifteen of those years and we've had three other beloved pooches since then. They've all adored their Dad. The fur kids sure know how to pick 'em, and so does God.

So I prayed a postscript, and got the husband and the dog. But not in that order.

# Touched by God
## MIRANDA DE JAGER

## 14 SEPTEMBER 1995

*O*n our tenth wedding anniversary I woke up at first light, not on an exotic island like Mauritius as we planned but alone in our queen-sized bed. I did not sleep well; I never do when I'm alone. I've had this problem since childhood but, since marrying, my sleep patterns improved. We lived in a normal suburb in a large town approximately 145 km east of Johannesburg. We had security doors and bars on all opening windows, because loitering and break-ins were common in our area. I have always been afraid of being alone, especially at night, even in the days before security became a serious problem in South Africa.

I'm a morning person and rise early to do Bible study or write in my journal. That day I remained in bed and prayed. I felt sad because on this anniversary our life was a shambles. We dreamed of celebrating it in style. Not that we could afford it, because business ventures had bombed.

We both worked hard in permanent jobs at a large steel manufacturing corporation before we decided to start a business. We didn't have children and built pipe-dreams about an affluent business to afford a new house and occasional overseas travels. We hatched a business idea, completed the research, saw a consultant and took the leap. Funds were tight but we arranged a second mortgage on our little 3-bedroom, 1-bathroom house.

Let's fast-track through a saga of rental premises in a shopping centre that was still under construction; buying expeditions in Johannesburg to acquire stock for our exciting endeavour that piled up in our hundred-square-metre house, before the business property was available.

In May 1995 my husband resigned to start the business, while I retained my existing employment to supplement our income. We didn't notice the red flags when they appeared, like the late completion of the building project. When at last we moved in, the staircase and walkways were incomplete and restricted access to our shop. The shop was located so we did not receive sufficient exposure which resulted in poor sales, though we marketed as best we could. We learned that it takes time to establish a new business. We did not have sufficient funds to sustain the shop indefinitely so we closed the business after three months.

My husband needed a job. He found something he'd never done before and was sent on a two-week training course in Pretoria, 100 km from our home. We only had one car and, due to the lack of safe public transport in South Africa, he took it. I could safely catch the company bus to work and he came home over weekends.

On our wedding anniversary he was in and out of training sessions. We did not have mobile phones in those days, so after unsuccessful attempts to connect via landline I finally caught him before he left for dinner. We only had a few minutes, but could at least wish each other a happy anniversary. My heart was breaking because all our wonderful dreams were shattered.

I was also struggling with my health. A few years earlier I had suffered from heartburn and experienced occasional heart palpitations. A cardiologist performed tests, including a halter ECG that monitored my heart for 24 hours. He noticed occasional spikes in my heartbeat, but found nothing wrong with my heart. An endoscopy diagnosed mild ulceration in my oesophagus at the entrance to my stomach and I was given an antacid. The doctor prescribed an anti-depressant to alleviate the stress I was experiencing at work. I did not have a high pressure job, but had been victimised by a more senior colleague over a long period of time. She was so subtle that, while other people were puzzled by some of her actions, nobody realised the extent or severity of her behaviour towards me. I was shy, introverted and did not know how to stand up for myself. It became worse when my position was combined with another role that became vacant. My workload increased and I was now working in the Industrial Relations department where I often had to liaise closely with trade unions and shop stewards. Shop stewards are often inclined to be persistent and fight for the rights of their union members. Some demanded to use my phone, tried to pressure me into doing additional chores, or simply took over my office. This added stress to my growing workload and put me in a position where I had to learn to say, 'NO,' for the first time in my life.

I was reluctant to take an anti-depressant, due to my mother's history of addiction to prescription medications. The doctor assured me it wasn't addictive and convinced me to take it temporarily to give my stomach time to heal. I agreed, but stopped taking it after a month because I didn't like the way it made me feel. Around that time my husband and I started cycling regularly. The exercise alleviated my stress and my stomach condition improved.

A few weeks before our anniversary, I presented with severe pain in my side. The doctor confirmed that it wasn't appendicitis, but couldn't find the cause. A colonoscopy diagnosed a spastic colon and referred me to an Internist (general specialist) to determine treatment for my stomach conditions—the one affected the other. At the age of twenty-nine, I was prescribed four different medications I should take for the rest of my life. I was devastated because, since I was in primary school, I'd seen my mother taking a variety of prescription drugs for stress-related issues. I saw how her addictions changed her personality and affected our family life.

On this day that should have been a joyous celebration, I felt gloomy and concerned. A close friend phoned and asked if she could pick me up for the conference at church that night. I knew about the event, but wasn't planning to go. However I realised that it might lift my spirits, and agreed to accompany her.

In that year, 1995, many churches around the globe were affected by the Brownsville revival. It had started at the Brownsville Assemblies of God church in Pensacola, Florida, and had also spread to many churches in South Africa. At the time, a local evangelist visited our church to conduct a conference over the weekend, but it continued during the week and there were services every night. We saw many miracles and healings during this time.

In church that night, as the worship was coming to an end, the evangelist started praying for people. He mentioned that God showed him there is someone with spastic intestines.

In my heart I argued that it couldn't be me because only my colon was spastic not my other intestines. When he corrected himself and said spastic colon, I knew the invitation was for me. I had never met this man and there was no way he could have known my issues. In spite of fear and self-consciousness,

I went forward. When he prayed for me, I fell over. Someone caught me, laid me down gently on the carpet and covered my legs like they did in those days. I could feel a heavy presence of God and while I was lying on my back, my knees started shaking. The shaking moved up from my knees to my body, my arms and hands. I felt myself taking deep breaths continuously. Tears ran down my face. I felt amazing joy. God's presence was so tangible I just wanted more of Him. I had an overwhelming desire to praise God. Jesus was doing a deep cleansing of my innermost being. When I moved my head, the room swirled. I have never been drunk in my life, as I do not use alcohol, but I can imagine that must be what it would feel like. My eyes were closed, but I was fully aware of what was happening. Occasionally I felt someone gently touching my forehead or my feet—they were praying for me. I wondered why my body shook and then knew that God was healing my colon.

The evangelist preached, but I can't remember what he said. As the singers started to sing again, I felt the Holy Spirit moving. The service was coming to an end and I did not want to keep my friend waiting, but I struggled to get up. When I managed to sit up, I felt dizzy. The room was spinning. I blinked a few times and remained seated for a while until the dizziness subsided.

After he closed the service, the evangelist walked over to me, spoke about an anointing of fire and said that I will never be the same again. In that moment I knew that God had touched me and healed my colon. I felt light and happy and experienced so much love. As I got to my feet, I still felt a little shaken, so my friend put her arm around my shoulders as we walked to the car. That night I slept like a baby. I did not need the medication anymore and my symptoms were gone.

During the next months, the pain in my side sometimes returned, but I knew that the enemy often does this to break down our faith. I rebuked him and thanked God for the healing He had given me. Every time I did that, the pain disappeared. Months later when we visited my husband's brother, his wife mentioned someone who cannot drink coffee, due to a spastic colon. Something clicked in my brain. I loved coffee, but hadn't been able to drink it since my teens because it gave me severe stomach ache. I started drinking coffee again and, to this day, it has never affected my stomach again.

Even though God healed my colon, we still had financial difficulties. My husband was working long hours in his new job that didn't pay much. One morning before work, about two months later, while I was reading my Bible, I prayed about our dire financial situation. At that point our monthly debt repayments, even without living costs, were more than our combined earnings. It was not sustainable and we needed a quick solution. As I prayed earnestly, my eyes fell on a Scripture in my open Afrikaans Bible. In that translation I read: *'The glory of this house will be greater than the former, says the Lord of Hosts. And in this place I will provide peace...'* (Haggai 2:9) I underlined it in my Bible, but was reluctant to share it with my husband in case it wasn't really from God. Yet the Lord is gracious and faithful over His word, even when our faith is weak.

Soon after, my husband phoned a company regarding a position he had applied for, but hadn't heard back from. The gears shifted and he was offered a position in his line of work. He started the new job a few weeks later, in December 1995. The salary was more than he had ever earned before. Then he met a senior person from another company who provided him with private work he could do from home in his spare time to supplement his income. There was a remarkable improvement in our financial situation. We settled our debts and improved our mortgage repayments. When we sold the house, we made enough profit to build a beautiful house in a more affluent neighbourhood.

In January 1996, on my 30th birthday, I realised I wasn't getting younger and decided to start studying. I'd always wanted a career, but had never had the opportunity to go to university after leaving school. I was an administrative officer at the time, but frustrated by the mundane nature of my work. My company's study aid scheme enabled me to follow a correspondence course towards my IT Diploma. By the grace of God, this was my first step towards a successful IT career, which assisted us many years later in our visa application towards immigrating to Australia.

I still marvel at the amazing gift God gave me when He touched me on our tenth wedding anniversary. God cares about every detail of our lives. Special days that are important to us are also important to Him, because He loves us dearly. God's touch has affected my life more than I realised at the time. In only a few short months, God had supplied all our needs and blessed us in ways we never anticipated.

# God's Protective Hands

## HAZEL BARKER

Colin found his sanctuary in the vast expanse of the Australian outback where the horizon kisses the earth. His father, Albert, a man of the soil, introduced him to the rhythms of farm life, where the cycles of sowing and reaping were as natural as breathing.

The simple joys of rural existence filled his days. He learned the art of patience, driving tractors in straight rows across fields that stretched into infinity. The farmhands, weathered and wise, became his unlikely teachers, imparting lessons not found in books but written in the lines of their hands.

The farm was his playground, his school, and his window to the soul of the land.

As he grew, so did his responsibilities. The farm turned from a playground to a workplace. The joy of bringing day-old lambs to shelter mingled with the sorrow of witnessing nature's unforgiving side. The hardships of farm life, the flock's struggles, and the shearing sheds' frenzied pace were all chapters in his story. But through it all, the land shaped his spirit which remained unbroken, like clay in the potter's hands.

Colin enjoyed watching the shearers compete. Some tried too hard and nicked the sheep, dyeing the white wool with red spots. After the shearing, the shearers covered the spots with tar to heal their wounds.

Johnnie, an indigenous boy with a heart as innocent as a newborn lamb's, was one of the top shearers. After tending the sheep, he would ask if anyone needed a haircut and would give a free haircut with the same shears he'd used on the sheep. Colin once joined the men for a haircut. He was afraid of being nicked by the shears, but Johnnie did as good a job as any barber. Johnnie's energy seemed boundless, for after dinner, the children gathered around him and listened to his stories. Colin never forgot his favourite tale, *Why Kangaroos Have Black Paws*, and many other dreamtime stories.

Albert and his son enjoyed country life, but living in a caravan and moving from place to place was particularly hard for Colin's mother, Ester. It restricted her to such a degree that she suffered from mood swings. One day she was the best of mothers; the next day, she'd throw Colin out of the van and yell, 'Clear off.'

The bush was the boy's solace, his guardian. He found comfort among the whispering eucalyptus and the rustling underbrush. The bush was a living tapestry, woven with the vibrant threads of lizards basking in the sun, goannas scaling the rough bark of trees, and grass snakes slithering through the undergrowth.

Yet the bush was more than a refuge to Colin; it stood as a witness to his growth from a boy who chased lizards to a man who understood the delicate balance of life. The caravan was home, and school was all but forgotten.

Ester had applied for her son to continue his studies by correspondence, and Albert made sure his son learned the work prior to answering the questions. 'Otherwise, you'll be digging ditches or emptying the nightsoil when you grow up,' he said.

When Albert was too busy to supervise Colin's work, Ester would send the answers in, provided he wrote something. 'Just copy the answers out of the book. What do I care?' she said.

Albert and Ester lived like gypsies, moving around from place to place. It was a confusing but consolidating time, as Colin learned about the bush and its occupants; where he became a country bumpkin, as his wife jokingly calls him.

'You can take the man from the bush, but not the bush from the man,' he said.

To this day, even though Colin no longer lives in the bush, its influence has never left him.

After several months of wandering around in the Victorian bush, returning every one or two weeks to their home in Portland, Albert finally gave in to Ester's pleadings and returned to Portland. Colin was glad to be back near the sea he loved. His mother enrolled him into the Portland Primary School.

On the first day of school, as Colin entered the grounds, the dust was kicked up by hundreds of feet, and the excited yells of boys reached him. In the classroom, the salty whiff of the ocean replaced the unfamiliar smell of newly sharpened pencils and books.

At playtime the school bully picked on him. 'Pommy bastard,' he shouted.

Some shoved and pushed him until he lost balance and fell. Many imitated his clumsy run. They yelled, 'Catch me if you can,' and ran off. Screaming with derision, they sped away, looking back to check whether he'd take up the challenge. Others lay on the ground and rolled with laughter.

Colin thought he'd die of shame. His breathing came in short, hurried gasps. His heart quivered with pain and suppressed sobs. He swallowed the hard lump in his throat and clenched his teeth. School was a nightmare. The iron gates and high brick walls made him feel like a prisoner. He missed the open green pastures and the quiet of the bush.

Because of Colin's disrupted studies in the bush, his teacher sent him to have his reading and spelling skills tested with a Guidance Counsellor.

The Guidance Counsellor was a Scot. 'How many "Rs" are there in rabbit?' he asked, pinning him with his eye. A Scottish burr stuck in his throat, and he rolled his 'Rs'.

Colin fidgeted while the counsellor held him at rapier point. The long drawn-out 'R' made him think there was more than one 'R' in rabbit. His answer was short and to the point. 'Several,' he replied, thinking they were too many to count.

The Counsellor put him in a special class.

Colin hated school and sometimes played truant, although he received a thrashing whenever found out. Classes were large, up to fifty children in a class. He sat at the back of the class while the teacher stood way up in front the whole day, drawing and writing things on the blackboard. Things the boy could not see or understand, so he lost interest and created a world where he wandered on the beach or in the bush, listening to the cries of whipbirds and butcher birds, and the louder cries of parrots, owls, and sulphur-crested cockatoos.

Colin only enjoyed music lessons at school, because his music teacher could look at the mundane and reveal the beauty, just as he looked at the bush and saw the Hand of the Creator.

One day, on a visit to the Melbourne Show, Colin's parents bought him ten volumes of *The Children's Encyclopaedia* by Arthur Mee. They became his prized possession. A few short hours reading brought the arts, the philosophy, and history of the world to life. He enjoyed spending hours with books, learning about amazing things and amassing knowledge. The author set problems, and unlike Colin's teachers, helped the reader. Captivated by the illustrations, the boy's inquiring mind wanting to delve further, began his reading journey.

Books opened a window of life to him, and he peered through with a wildly beating heart. On rainy days, he curled up in bed with a book, listening to the full frog symphonies and developing the delightful habit of reading. A precocious child with a retentive memory and an insatiable thirst for knowledge, it got him out of his mother's hair, and he no longer fretted on rainy days when restrained from enjoying the outdoors.

On his ninth birthday, Colin received a Meccano set from his parents. He enjoyed the thrill of being able to build things, to watch the motors rotate and the gears whirl. Mechanics never ceased to fill him with wonder.

He read during playtime at school. It formed a protective barrier between him and the others, forming an insurmountable wall like a fortress. He was mentally alert and active, achieving satisfaction from the store of knowledge he accumulated from the school library and Arthur Mee's encyclopaedia. Books also taught him to regard things from a different perspective. Colin never forgot the hurt he suffered during his first months at school when bullying had occupied a large part of his school days and much of his dreams at night. Books provided a refuge from the distress of hurt and pain. His leaden lips refused to give voice to his hurt, but he used sarcasm as a weapon in defence of himself.

He often came up with bright ideas and witty comments. He saw the humorous side of episodes and used his sense of humour to make acerbic comments on others. The pen is sharper than the sword, but his tongue made sharp cuts too.

Divine intervention must have smiled on him since, despite all the drawbacks, he achieved average results at school. Colin remained a testament to the enduring spirit of the Australian bush—a man whose heart had been forged in solitude but filled with the quiet majesty of the land.

God's protective Hand remained over him, shielding him from the taunts of his schoolmates and the pitfalls of life.

# A Sign — Disguised Blessings

## DIANA DAVISON

The new year started off unpredictably unpleasant: a painful snow-skiing accident in January during our overseas family holiday. This debilitating incident resulted in enduring reconstructive surgery. A left reverse total shoulder replacement. From that point on, my husband became my driver, bag carrier, food provider and, most importantly, sweet tea maker. Taking time out to adjust to my predicament took some getting used to. The challenge of being sling-bound for two months tested my imagination during nights of insomnia. Sleeping, showering, dressing—all turned into taxing tasks performed in slow motion. And my wiry bird's nest hair… secondary in the scheme of things. I learned proficiency at one-handed cap and hairband donning and relished the once-a-week scalp wash at the beauty salon.

The shift into neutral and parked didn't come easy for me. I spent many hours in my study stationary with my overactive mind exercising on what needed to get done when I became more able. All pending projects required two hands. And permanently placed on my conscience sat my 86-year-old mother. The physical state of my body is fixable. My mother's situation is irreversible, no matter what. The stage IV cancer remains her unshakable dark shadow. It had been nearly five months since my last Borneo venture, where she lives. After being reliant on those around me to help me heal, the time had arrived to go see her. A trip to reconnect.

With the surgeon's approval when the sling came off, I flew overseas. I journeyed to visit my frail mother solo. I had paused my commitments and plans far too long and was keen to get going. Four weeks seemed to be an adequate period to slowly build strength, confidence and to get used to being two-armed again. I left Brisbane airport with trepidation and excess mind baggage. My head cluttered with uncertainties. *Will my shoulder hold up? Do I bring a sling just in case?* (I did—a couple of different types.) *Will I manage confidently in and out of taxis with my luggage? Will it be the rainy season? I can't afford to fall.* Jousting questions, noisy and never-ending. I had to brush them aside. I told myself: *You got this. Things will work out. I'll be ok. Move forward with faith.*

The travel from Brisbane to Kuala Lumpur (KL) via Adelaide was comfortable enough. I sought an extra pillow and had ample assistance to place my backpack in the overhead compartment. There was a slight delay, allowing me to settle in and pick movies to watch. But upon arriving in KL, the earlier delay created a manic rush. I had to navigate my way over to the next terminal through immigration and a bus ride. It was important to arrive at the designated gate early and not miss my onward flight. I hurried as best I could. My light luggage and old sneakers got me to the finish line with twenty minutes to spare, sweat trickling down my back. An unplanned but needed workout.

The connecting airplane arrived at my final destination at 7:30 pm. The City of Kuching, Sarawak, is a semi-sleepy and pleasant place with a non-congested airport, efficient immigration booths and straightforward baggage retrieval. Regardless, I did not expect to stand for thirty minutes waiting for my luggage. The suitcase was absent. The conveyor belt snaked empty. On tired feet, I approached the customer service counter armed with questions. The sympathetic ground personnel didn't receive many complaints. They instantly focused their attention. One person surveyed the moving belt while the other staff member tapped her keyboard to track down my belongings. The story unfolded. I flew to KL via Adelaide using the carrier Qantas, then proceeded on Malaysian Airways (MAS). The unforeseen came about when Qantas winged my carryall on an aircraft through to Sydney instead… strange. This mistake placed everything out of sync. After understanding this, I had the freedom to leave the airport. My only carry was a small haversack in hand. So easy.

I was assured the airline would forward the missing luggage on a later flight and deliver it to me. I caught a taxi to the hotel where staff awaited my arrival. When I pulled up outside, an employee greeted me warmly, holding open the front door, ready to take any bags. 'Thanks, but no suitcase,' I announced. Undeterred, he grabbed my rucksack and followed me inside. Many helping hands were eager to assist. During the wait, the chill of cold beer was a cheer. Not much I could do, but… just relax. My main bag finally arrived four hours later—carried directly up the stairs of the hotel to the reception area. The only effort left for me, wheeling it straight to the lift and on to my air-conditioned room. So easy.

During this short ten-day sojourn an unexplored rollercoaster of emotions unfurled. A tense ride of more downs than ups. My mother had not been feeling well two days prior to my surprise trip to see her. My initial entrance into her bedroom at the care home residence did not result in the happiest of reunions. The only face emanating brightness belonged to the bunch of flowers I gave her. I worried daily if this marked the beginning of the end. And my constant companion… questions. *Will she deteriorate during my stay? Will I need to change my return flight? Is it a virus or the cancer? Are these the effects of the regular oral doses of morphine?* My spirit felt incredibly down, but I had to rise above it all to give her strength. I needed her to recover. All the while, I continued to attempt shoulder-strengthening exercises in the confines of my hotel room. In this private space, I allowed myself to cry. Helpless tears to a hopeless situation.

I did my best to stay centred, dedicating each afternoon to visiting my mother. I never knew what scene would present itself until I walked through her bedroom door. In each taxi ride to see her, apprehension lay heavy on my broken shoulder. More questions. *Would she be just resting or in deep sleep with eyes closed and mouth open? Would her hearing be on low volume and her memory teetering even lower on the edge of blurriness? Would she understand my chattering or would I need to repeat myself in explanation over and over and over? Would she fall into slumber again as I was talking, my voice a lullaby?* I prayed she would be awake and my visits would revive her.

Any enjoyable sittings were infrequent, but I was patient, waiting for her smile to greet me. She eventually stayed conscious long enough to hear my news, sometimes attempting to return conversation. The trip neared its end. My mother started turning a corner. Two days before I departed, she began dining in the communal space with the other residents. The visit to see her before my flight to Australia the next day held special moments. I sat with her during dinner. We watched a muted show about coconut farmers. Then, inside her bedroom, we looked over old black and white photographs. We even shared a giggle at my one-handed selfie taking session. I left my mother's home facility in a sunny mood. A sense of relief draped over me. I felt blessed at being granted time with her and able to observe her revert to a better state and her former self again.

On the last day, I headed out to the airport late afternoon, although I was booked for an 8:30pm departure. I looked forward to appreciating the lounge, a quiet Tiger beer to reflect on my journey and… just relax. A ping on my phone soon interrupted me. MAS made an announcement regarding a schedule change of 45 minutes. A delay. It made timing tight for my onward connection out of KL and onto Australia. Again, I found myself at a service counter relaying my itinerary to gain confirmation I would not miss my international flight. The airport was experiencing higher-than-normal levels of crowding. The earlier flights got cancelled because of the volcano eruption in Indonesia's Mount Ruang. I had to wait, but the friendly customer support team assured me, 'Don't worry, madam. We have alerted the ground staff. There will be someone there to assist you through the terminal. You are one of five passengers that need to connect onwards.'

Eventually, I boarded my flight, hiding my hand luggage under a blanket as I took my seat. I did not want to extend myself trying to place it in the overhead compartment. Upon arrival at KL, a MAS representative waited to expedite travellers with onward destinations. I was the last passenger to board the international aircraft. However, this plane was also kept on hold—a wait on the supply of bottled water. Another delay. This allowed me to settle down for the long haul home and… just relax.

Various interruptions of transit are usually not welcome on any journeys. Previously, MAS flew direct after the post-pandemic gates of restricted travel opened up. Then things changed. Flights were cancelled or delayed. Airlines no longer fly direct as they did before. Bustling Sydney is now a first point of entry for immigration. The streamlined experience I hoped for was dashed as I collected my luggage, and rechecked it for a connecting flight home. Surrounding me was an undulating sea of people all following signs—verbal, written or arrowed. People shuffled along, to the constant hum of wanderers, young and old. Voices interrupted over the tannoy in muffled tones of English spoken in random spurts of clarity. Announcements were hard to decipher. The diverse traffic of travellers seemed to move in a holding pattern.

I made my way to baggage claim, waiting with all the other passengers cleared by immigration. After a long lag, I stood alone. A solitary passenger without luggage to collect. The carousel was empty, ready for the next load of ferried belongings. Another delay. And so, I made my way to customer service. They confirmed that my bag had not been loaded onto the flight. It was AWOL again… strange. I looked at my phone app 'Find My' and saw that my suitcase remained sitting in KL. The ground staff member swiftly completed a form then I slotted myself into a different queue and headed on through to clearance. I was grateful I had been spared the inconvenience of collecting my 14 kg case and attempting to lift it at various stages.

On my final domestic leg back to Brisbane, I occupied a window seat with my hand luggage once more concealed at my feet. I put my headphones on and drifted off, glad to be heading home. All that awaited me was a walk off the plane and straight through into a waiting taxi. So easy.

The following day, I dispatched emails about my missing bag. By 2 pm, I had received no update. The first flight out of Sydney did not have my belongings. The 'Find My' app indicated my bag to have been in KL and later transported to Sydney, but not at the airport. I sent off screenshots and messages, receiving welcome rapid responses to my queries. They scheduled the delivery in the evening between 7–11 pm. A wide window to watch out for. I wondered how many missing pieces of luggage needed to be returned to their owner before I got mine.

Earlier that day, driving back to my place from physiotherapy, I was listening to a radio show in my car. I had missed its start so wanted to hear it again—*Learning to Live Out God's Call in Your Life*. Once home, I accessed the show's website to replay the broadcast from the beginning. I clicked play. Then, at that precise moment, on that particular afternoon, I lifted my head to gaze out of the living room glass-screen. I was utterly awestruck. A sign displayed in broad daylight. I got up and walked closer to the large windowpane. With my mobile phone in hand, I quickly attempted to capture the spectacular scene before me.

It was a magnificent vision. But the photograph did not do justice to the significant symbol. The picture image seemed less dynamic, humble even. I realised the occurrence had to be witnessed while it existed, committed to memory. A dazzling display of radiance permeating over rooftops. I understood sunlight had bounced off a reflective surface and would vanish within seconds. But what mesmerised me, shining across the river into my line of sight, was truly breathtaking. All I could express was... WOW! The rainbow-like layers that shimmered off each four tips acted like a shield to frame the cross. The visual travelled into my house and into heart.

Through all the uncertainty and unavoidable struggle, a guiding force remained present. There was no need to fear. My sobs and sighs, the babble of thoughts and prayers, had all been heard and acknowledged. The positive progress in my mum's poor health soothed my suffering before I left her. I found the serenity to accept the inevitability of things I certainly could not change. It all fell outside of my control. But I was still able to be there for my mother. And what are the odds of my suitcase not being on the same flight as me— twice? Throughout this trip, I had support along the way, seen and not seen. Help was always close by. The setbacks and stalls were disguised blessings. My bag ended up being the first on the lost luggage list, delivered straight to my door with stickers stating *Priority* and *Rush* stuck to it. My only effort was to wheel it into my home. So easy.

And the two just-in-case slings originally packed for the journey—well, they thankfully stayed out of arms' way.

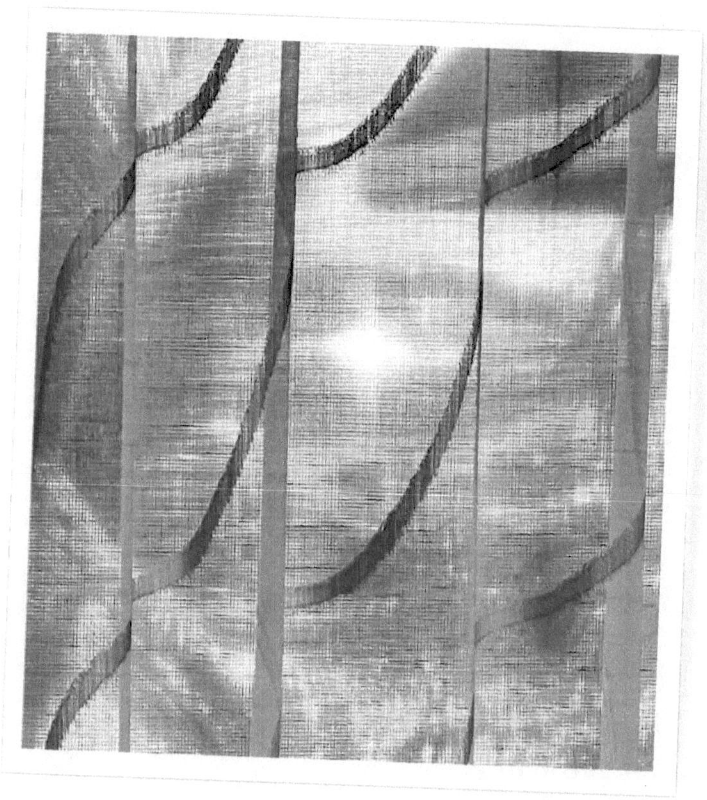

A SIGN — DISGUISED BLESSINGS (23 APRIL 2024)

# Twenty-Seven Years
## MICHELLE DENNIS EVANS

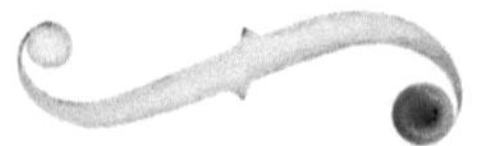

Nine thousand eight hundred and fifty-five days
shared breaths and intertwined dreams
a love that has been bent over and over
but refuses to break.

I trace the deepening laugh lines
marvel at our tapestry
woven with threads of triumph
shadows of defeat
battles fought to overcome darkness
victories celebrated in light.

Not a fairytale
but maybe more beautiful
for every imperfection.
Our broken alabaster jar
spilling grace through its cracks,
a fragrance of forgiveness
overshadowed with grace and love.

We came carrying impossible dreams,
clutching childhood fairytales,
expecting knights in armour,
mind-readers and perfection,
while excusing our own flaws
like scattered pieces of a puzzle.

Judgment marking failures
neither measuring up.
Years and tears taught us—
beautifully broken humans,
was our imperfect love.
Admission, let us breathe,
our marriage revived, survived.

Wearing masks
our new expectation,
dimmed in who we were,
dreams swallowed like stones,
yet still attempting to dance
to unspoken rhythms
a mirror of unfulfillment.

But oh—
when we stopped reaching for perfection
we bloomed like wildflowers through concrete.
His never-ending dad jokes
my belt-out-a-tune kitchen songs
two distinct instruments in God's orchestra
sometimes in harmony
sometimes striking wrong notes
synchronised as uniquely us.

Choosing to champion
Each other's dreams
Marriage is an adventure
Free to be messy, loud
strong yet vulnerable.

The seven-year itch isn't a myth
we've felt it come and go
testing all the love we know.
First family and career
played tug-of-war
young family strains
and growing pains.

At fourteen the world crowded in
drowning us in busyness.
Yet through the chaos we swam
surfacing stronger together.

Twenty-one flitted by
far gentler than expected.
Perhaps new rhythms played in tune
as we enjoyed our children grow
caught in their ambitions and dreams
taxiing them to and fro.

The choice to hold on
as we watched others let go
refining moments
through each itch
called us to love deeper
keeping God at the centre.

We walk beaches to reset
steal weekends in mountain air
dance under cruise ship stars
invest in our marriage
like it's the most valuable asset we own
our desire to win at love.

And here we are at twenty-seven
not completing, or competing
but championing.
Creating space for wings to spread
watching each other soar
into divine purpose.
Two melodies in God's symphony
more beautiful for being broken
more precious for being real.
Purpose embraced
our bond deepened
a fulfillment beyond words.

# Life with Dad

## JO WANMER

Barefoot I raced across the dirt road. No need to look for cars as they rarely passed our house. They could be heard from a mile away. If I'd thought a car was coming, I'd be sitting in the concrete pipe under the road. In my mind spiders were safer than strangers.

Instead of cars I could hear the steady lowing of cows and the occasional crack of a stock whip. Dad was nearly home. I'd pleaded to ride with him and help muster the cattle. However school was higher on Dad's priority list, so I'd rocked my chair in the school room instead of plodding behind the dust on my pony. School work was easy and soon completed. Now I was free.

I raced past the turkey nest—an earthen structure that stored water, not eggs—and dodged the bad patch of bindi-eye without too much prickle-damage to my feet. I swerved into the machinery shed to scan for snakes. Sometimes I'd see one there but none caught my eye today. Out the back door of the shed, I climbed onto the top of the post-and-rail fence and shaded my eyes, squinting into to the western sun. I could see the cloud of dust but not the lead cows.

Grabbing a breath, I decided there was enough time to walk the rails. Arms out for balance I raced from one post, along the top rail—an old skinny tree trunk—to the next post. Eight rails down the yard, turn at the corner and five rails across. Now I was above the water trough that would soon be mobbed by cows. Jumping down, I wrestled the chain holding the gate. Lifting it off its hook I rode the gate as it swung open.

I raced back down the fence far enough so the large red animals weren't spooked by my presence. Perched on a big post, I pulled prickles out of my calloused feet and waited for Dad. The mob pushed through the gate into the yard. Dad rode on my side of the wall of the cattle. Once close to me, he steered the horse beside my post and I slipped on behind him, arms clinging to his spare frame.

Mine was an idyllic childhood with endless acres of bush, countless cattle and horses. I remember the day Dad bought his first tractor. I could barely imagine it when he told me. But soon I was driving it everywhere. Down to change the irrigation lines. Through the house paddock to bring in the cows at sunset. We'd lock the calves up overnight and next morning milk their mothers. It never was a chore. At about sun-up, Dad would pull his three kids' bedroom windows open from the outside. 'Who'd like to come milking with me?' The others rarely responded but I loved to be with Dad and went at every opportunity.

We lived in an amusement park. As well as walking on top of fences, my brother and I balanced on the sides of empty petrol drums and 'walked' them down the road to the grid and then back up again. After a lot of practice, I could balance as I steered the drum across the cattle grid. There was the turkey nest to swim in and leeches to pull off when we climbed out. The windmill was out of bounds, but that didn't stop us climbing it when mum was occupied. We gathered eggs, helped in the veggie garden and played for hours in the dirt under the house, building roads and towns out of mud.

Occasionally we'd go to town to shop, and on Sundays we went to church. But we never knew what it was like to eat at the only café in town. The only ice-cream we knew was the home-made variety, and we remained unaware there were other options.

As a family we ate beef, home-slaughtered and butchered. Stew was my favourite breakfast, though Mum preferred eggs and Dad cooked porridge. Cold meat for lunch and hot roast for dinner was standard fare. We didn't know any other food except when we drove two days to visit Mum's mother. There we played with cousins, swam in pools without leeches, and discovered such delicacies as sausages and bacon!

Bread came twice a week with the mailman. Fruit and potatoes arrived the same way, having been picked up off the train.

If the fruit was old and soft, it was stewed and eaten with custard or cream. We 'separated' the milk from the cream every morning and then made butter using the Mixmaster. When seasons and water allowed, we picked vegetables from the garden or tipped them out of tins. Desserts and cakes appeared from the wood-burning stove. Yes, to me it was the best life.

By the time I had to leave home and start regular school instead of correspondence school, I was strong, independent and a quick thinker. My brother and I lived with an elderly lady in town. She cut our lunches and cooked dinner but otherwise we looked after ourselves. We had the whole town to explore. Trainlines, saleyards and showgrounds were all within running distance. Mum and Dad were easy to contact via phone. Mum arrived in town every Friday to drive us home for a weekend of fun for us and washing and ironing for her.

Dad always taught us, training us in the ways of the land. But his dreams for us were much bigger than working in dust behind cattle, struggling through drought and flood, fighting fires in searing heat, and shooting pigs and kangaroos that decimated his precious grass. We knew how to plant wheat, brand cattle, shoot a rifle and spray weeds—but Dad wanted us at university to expand our choices and opportunities.

We could drive every vehicle on the property. The prerequisite was leg-strength. As soon as we could push the clutch down, we were allowed to drive it. We were trained in direction, expected to find our own way through the trees and to work out answers to problems. If we asked Dad what we should do, he'd reverse the question. 'What do you think is the best plan?' He always taught us how to make decisions rather than supply the answer. On the flipside he expected unquestioning obedience to his requests. He encouraged us to learn at every opportunity. 'Why don't you enter this category in the show?' He pointed to the Children's section — *Best Selection of Grasses*. Who knew there were over a hundred different grasses on our land?

His life was a constant example. He loved our mother unceasingly, even when she was crabby. In his tiny office he poured over figures or his Bible. Glasses pulled down his nose, he'd always stop to chat or give a quick hug. Some Sundays he preached from the high pulpit in our old church. Occasionally Mum would play the organ. God was a given, a permanent part of our life... the same as beef and milking.

Some nights Mum would gather us around the piano to sing hymns. We enjoyed it but soon turned it into a game. Piano lessons at the convent happened as soon as we went to town. Scales, daily practice and practical exams followed under the instruction of a crusty old nun.

Dad served the community... on the show committee, secretary of the Graziers Association, and then a Councillor of the Shire. He knew so many people that visitors were frequent. Though I kept my distance, I still learned hospitality. Once a month all our neighbours arrived at our home for a church service held on our veranda. Afterwards there was afternoon tea and adult conversation. For us kids it was the highlight of our lives to have friends to play with.

By the time I left for boarding school, I could single-handedly move the long line of spray pipes and turn the handle on the massive diesel motor. I'd watch as the water flooded the lucerne. Blocked sprays had to be cleared, a tricky job when there was frost all over the ground and ice hanging from the wire fences. I would go with dad's employed men and muster a paddock or help to pull a trapped cow from a bog-hole. Using the tractor we'd drag a dead beast over to the 'butchering' tree.

We were expected to help in the kitchen and turn the handle on the rollers that squeezed the water out of the washed clothes. But these were chores. Activities outside with dad were fun.

Then it was time…

Mum and Dad drove me to Rockhampton and a new life began. Boarding school! There were only fifteen boarders in my year eleven cohort. We slept in one vast room above our classrooms. Each girl was allocated a bed and a chest of drawers. We shared one walk-in-robe and a massive bathroom. This open community living was difficult for some but, to me, it was a window into a new world. In the classroom some girls were smarter than me. In my tiny class at home in year ten, I'd worked enough to keep me on the top, win most of the prizes. Now, in year eleven, lessons became more challenging.

But the people! Some girls lived a life I'd never heard of. They gloated about fast cars, boyfriends and excesses as they rehashed their school holidays. A few girls were as conservative and sheltered as I was. There were three terms a year. The only time I saw Dad and Mum was in the holidays. To get home, we caught a train, unsupervised. We had four girls to a compartment, each with pull-down beds so we could sleep—not that many did. The train also carried the students from the boys' school. For twelve hours we jumped from compartment to compartment and terrorised the guards. After a term of total confinement, freedom was heady. The train was where I felt restricted by my father's instructions. Here I had to choose my behaviour. His guidance ran deep and I often chose sleep as the safest option.

My body started to develop. I'd thought I was going to look like a boy forever. Sudden changes were difficult to navigate without parental input. We had no access to a phone. Ever. Mum wrote twice a week, a letter ready to go with every train. I'd write back and ask questions but the answers were always a week away. By then, I'd have different queries. Dad wrote too, but not as regularly. Mum's letters were about daily happenings. Dad's letters were more conversational. In his scrawly writing, he commented on news, using other people's stories to instruct me in life, or talk about God. On one occasion, having to decide the timing of music exams, I wrote and asked him what I should do, eagerly awaiting his answer. In his reply he wrote a strategy for persuading my music teacher to agree with me and talked of his confidence I would make the best decision. His answer left me frustrated. I wanted him to instruct me. But not my dad. He continued to push me towards independence.

I wonder as I look back if he knew. Was he using every opportunity to train me, knowing his time was short?

One message, given to me after dinner by the school matron, changed my life. 'Your father has had a heart attack.' No more information was offered. All I could do was walk away. Even under those circumstances, there was no access to the phone. No more details. I crawled into bed numb. The next day I was sent home, flying in a plane for the first time. The plane carried four other relatives. Clearly my daddy was seriously unwell.

Three weeks later, the bottom fell out of our world. Dad was found dead in his hospital bed.

How does a ship continue to sail without a rudder? How does one continue to breath when the light of your life is snuffed out? For two weeks I tried to help and comfort my bereft mother, but then I was back on the train, for to lose more schooling would have been unthinkable. Dad wanted me there. He wanted me to earn entry to university.

Not only did I lose my beloved dad, our home and property had to be sold. Our entire lifestyle was lost. Mum bought an old fibro house in town. Never painted. Toilet cleared by a night cart. My brother and I painted the inside of that house during the summer holidays. Mum's colour choice? Grey. Had we ever painted before? No, but we were dad's kids, trained to believe we could do anything. So we did. The frustration came in getting to the house from the farm. Neither of us were old enough to have a driver's licence, and as much as we pleaded, Mum wouldn't let us drive alone.

Soon I was back on the train to return to school. By the time I came home next holidays, everything had been sold. My horse, my home, my tractor, my cows and my lifestyle had all disappeared under the auctioneer's hammer. I couldn't run the dusty tracks or climb the stacks of bailed hay to check my initials carved on the timbers of the roof. I returned to an unfamiliar, crowded bedroom surrounded by grey walls with an outside dunny.

But I'd been trained by an amazing father to make the best of everything. So, I did what I could to help a greyed-out, exhausted mother.

A year later I travelled alone by train to Brisbane. After twelve hours to Rockhampton, I waited at a friend's house and then travelled another twelve hours to Brisbane. With no one to meet me, I caught a cab to the accommodation Mum had organised — a Presbyterian College for Girls.

Now there was a whole city to discover! But I missed my brother, my exploring companion. I found my way to university. Others from school were there, but not doing my course. I walked into the biggest lecture room I'd seen in my life. Where to sit? I chose a seat beside another girl who looked lost… like me. As we chatted, I discovered she was a Christian, conservative and smart. And I knew that Dad's prayers had preceded me. His training steadied me. His plan for my life was being fulfilled.

I never did finish that degree, because I was floating without a rudder. Dad's voice wasn't there to keep me steady. Mum moved to Brisbane a year later, gathering all her children under one roof. Christmas morning she ushered us all into a new church, full of life and youth. I met my husband there, a man who'd always wanted to marry the daughter of a farmer.

Fifty-four years later, I reflect and thank God for my wise father who taught and loved me well in the few years he was given.

# Wronged!

## MIRANDA DE JAGER

When I'm angry at being used,
manipulated, and abused.
The unfair turnout of my life,
caused by cruel selfish lies.
Betrayed by their respected disguise—
their dishonesty fooled even the wise.
I feel like crying, lashing out,
giving vent to a shout.
Yet I cannot retaliate,
it will never change my fate...

It affected my entire life,
caused me so much strife.
I carried all the guilt,
thought it was my fault!
Too young to know another's wrong,
they stole my innocence, my song.
Yet, if I lash out for my sake,

I'll be like them—flawed and fake.
How do I handle this with care,
why is life so unfair?

I prayed for God's grace over me,
I knew I had to forgive…
His perfect plan and His love,
changed my view to see above,
the brokenness I've carried for so long.
I took His hand—He made me strong.
I no longer feel so alone,
He understands my every groan.
My heavenly Father heard me pray,
I found His way—the only way!

# *Why Not?*

## RUTH BONETTI

*M*y addiction began in my early teens and continues to the present. Within seconds of playing music in a youth orchestra, I was hooked. The wave of surround sound washed me far beyond any horizons I could envision.

It was all the more electrifying for a child of the outback, raised on hillbilly music. I first heard the clarinet on ABC radio and resolved, 'I will learn to create that mellow sound.' We played Brahms' *Hungarian Dance* at a music camp under the baton of the visionary John Curro.

Early paths into the world music scene were forged by wand-brandishing 'Big JC', who fired his young musicians with enthusiasm, drive and vision. His irrefutable 'Why not?' would spur us to tackle pieces beyond our abilities.

John's side-kick collaborator, Franciscan friar Fidelis Stinson, buzzed around Brisbane on an instrument-laden scooter, his brown robes flapping. 'Father Fid' played a pivotal role heading the committee of Queensland Secondary Schools Music Teachers' Association to form a music festival orchestra of 94 players. Never mind the tentative ensemble and impure intonation, we played tutti with bravura. We breathed in unison. After a resounding first performance, players and their parents demanded more. And so the Queensland Youth Orchestra was born. And I, the shy outback loner, found my team in musical ensemble.

In those early days we rehearsed in schools, church halls, a West End theatre, a seedy nightclub the morning after. JC wielded a true adventurer's spirit of vision and faith—and the capacity to advance titanic crazy-brave goals with imagination and confidence. Like taking his six-year-old orchestra to perform in Italy and at the 1972 International Festival of Youth Orchestras in Lausanne, Switzerland.

JC persuaded sponsors, politicians and reluctant executive boards to support his mammoth goal. 'Why not?'

Potential backers were convinced an overseas tour was a feasible dream. Living through vision in action, this inspiring experience broadened my horizons and increased my own future confidence. And so it was that we embarked on an illuminating adventure, beginning with frenzies of fundraising, followed by manoeuvres to launch an orchestral caravan into the air. A constant flux of celli, tuba and their owners drifted around the Alitalia plane. The frazzled crew resorted to feeding us to keep us in our seats.

In Rome airport an exhausted mass of purple-clad bodies slumped—think Cooktown orchids, jacarandas, geddit?—sweating hotter than back home. (Why isn't Europe cold? I packed the wrong clothes.)

We straggled onto buses to head into the frenzied traffic, rounded a corner and *wham!* I was gobsmacked by my first sight of the Colosseum! I was there, right where Nero fiddled and Christians faced off against horrific brutality, martyred for their faith in public orgies of cruelty as these barbarians cheered their demise.

I've loved Ancient History since high school, and this first (somewhat...) real-live ruin blew my eyes up to my eyebrows. As did a visit to ancient catacombs. Where Christians hid underground from their Roman oppressors, groping their way with small oil lamps. As the Roman Empire crumbled... we can observe uncanny replicas in the present century.

Our big European debut neared in Lausanne. Would we be good enough? Insecurity and angst flared into blind funk from the top down. Our orchestral manager-cum-chaperone nudged me to 'say something' to a glum Maestro. Because our formidable big JC, the intrepid Pied Piper, was scared witless.

Why me? I wondered. True, I was a senior member of the orchestra. His nudge to me to support and encourage was a first step to writing books and giving presentations that encourage performance confidence. John's momentary insecurity propelled me into publishing the books, *Taking Centre Stage* and *Confident Music Performance.*

Big JC took an enormous faith step to launch a kid orchestra from provincial Queensland onto an international stage. But he paid the toll of self-doubt. Was he overwhelmed? Exhausted? Was it juggling the Aussie dollars with Italian lira? Communication problems perhaps? We noticed his morose, insecure manner. He had made a huge economic gamble, possibly risked his own house to his vision.

Relief at last came with resounding applause from both audience and critics. We could enjoy our second concert in the courtyard of Rolle Chateau; a lake cruise to Chillon Chateau; a dramatic lakeside *1812 Overture.*

As John said: 'In 10 days we went from thinking we were no-hopers to knowing exactly how we fitted into the international scene. We discovered we weren't the best orchestra, but by no means were we the worst.'

*Avanti* to ten heady days in Italy!

We lived it up—and down. Before our performance in Salo's piazza of the fourteenth-century cathedral our five-course feast was lubricated with molto vino. Euphoria and accelerated tempi. 'Stand up if you can,' Il Maestro grunted at the final cadence of Tchaikovsky's 5th *Symphony.* Did a misunderstanding over the tab see us in tents near Monza for our next few days?

Thousands-strong audiences loved our performances at Bergamo, the Pitti Palace in Florence, Sforza Castle in Milan—culminating with a memorable final performance in an exquisite theatre in Siena. We emerged to the *Palio* horse race through the city square, with its electric atmosphere of flag-waving and medieval costumes.

In the early decades of QYO, the players' enthusiasm compensated for lack of experience. Though one of the youngest orchestras to perform at Lausanne, with some members just 13, we Queenslanders returned home boosted by an international reputation, appreciated both as musicians and ambassadors.

I walked into Brisbane airport thinking, 'When and how can I return?'

*Why not?* So I did. My husband and I lived and worked in Europe for seven years.

The meteoric rise of professionalism, finesse and standard humbles early alumni who felt privileged to play in the fledgling orchestra. John Curro burst open the state cultural cringe with a Queensland orchestra that defied condescension.

My own teaching methods owe much to John's vision and challenges. Especially that he chose repertoire that stretched players to the edges of our seats. Could we achieve this? Somehow we did.

John was moist-eyed when I presented him with my book

*Sounds and Souls: How music teachers change lives* (as we know they do!) and read the dedication to him and to my clarinet teacher, David Shephard:

> *For two beacons who lit my voyage into music, teaching and indeed, life: David Shephard, who listened, encouraged, and whose sounds warmed my soul. John Curro, for opportunities, vision and the challenge of 'Why not?'*

We may think our appreciation of teachers and mentors but do we express it? A sentence of thanks, a card or a tribute can uplift teachers who did not realise the impact of words they long forget speaking.

How many others has the Maestro challenged outside their comfort zone to reach new heights? Thank you, John, for spurring me to excel, for your insight and inspiration. QYO changed my life. How could I have anticipated the impact of this, my first step into performance, but even more to writing books that encourage performers of both words and music? Many thousands more, professional musicians across Australia and internationally, and inspirational teachers, might echo my words from *Sounds and Souls:*

> *Wheels turn. Generations join the momentum. Many of the 8,000 and rising Alumni see their own children and grandchildren dance to John Curro's Pied Piper call of: 'Why not?'*

# Show Me ME

## ROSE DEE

The biggest struggle in my life has been with the spirit of rejection. Up until my mid-thirties, I didn't know rejection was the root cause of my problems—I just knew something was wrong with me. It was only when I petitioned God for understanding that the spirit of rejection was exposed. But the journey to revealing the source of rejection and its deep roots in my life and even my identity was a long journey of revelation. This great outworking of faith took me on a road to embracing who the Lord made me to be, not the person I had been made into. I came to understand the programming of my childhood and was rescued from the thought processes I had been conditioned to accept.

Rejection has many layers, and as each layer came to the surface and was healed, I thought it had to be the last one. From my mid-thirties, each layer was dealt with in God's perfect timing, but the layer I want to share in detail is the last layer—the layer that sealed my healing. This has happened in these last five years of my life.

As I write this, I am fifty years old. I was married for seventeen years and have now been a widow for five years, having nursed my husband through cancer until I lost him in 2019. I am still raising our son, who is now eighteen. When my husband passed, I felt like the only strength I had left was the knowledge that God was good and that He loved me. That was the only thing my mind, body, soul and spirit knew, and even that knowledge was weak. So, as I lived day by day in fight/flight/freeze mode, I had no confidence in any part of my identity to drive me forward. I was living in a heightened fight state, relying on adrenaline to propel me into 2020.

Then COVID hit, and my state of fight became a normality.

One year after my husband's passing, I was launched into a season that unravelled my life even further. I was completely abandoned by someone I had chosen to trust. But it was more than that. It felt cruel, incomprehensible, deeply confusing, and … familiar. At the same time, I suffered a bowel perforation and sepsis that, apart from a miracle of God, would have killed me. The rest of the year was spent in and out of hospital, but I had time to think and contemplate. What was it about me that had attracted that person? Why had I put up with and contributed to that treatment, and allowed it into my life? I petitioned the Lord for the answer.

'Show me ME' was my prayer, a prayer that led me on a deep journey of revelation to understanding and forgiving narcissistic abuse. You might ask, where was my support? Who did I have to lean on?

At this point, I need to introduce you to my childhood.

There's good, bad, and ugly in every family. I am not a psychiatrist or psychologist. I'm not even a therapist. I have no business diagnosing or judging anyone, and I don't want to. I fully forgive, so this is not an exercise in blame or character assassination. I just know that understanding narcissistic abuse was the beginning of my freedom from that last layer of rejection.

I was the middle child in my family. I look back now and realise I always felt like an outsider. As a youngster, I was excruciatingly shy. I had little to no self-esteem, and I don't recall expressing any strong individuality or rebellion. My opinion wasn't sought and, mostly, I knew not to offer it.

My emotional survival depended on several things: being pleasing, keeping up the appearance of goodness, and not making any strong personal demands. I was uninteresting. Honestly, for the most part, that was fine with me. I enjoyed my own company and the company of books. I had no real connection with members of my family except for one who died young. I was later to understand this disconnection within a family is a symptom of narcissistic abuse.

The only place I truly lived as a version of myself was in my imagination. There I was free from what I perceived as the grip of control and domination. But when your identity is attached to your imagination, it isn't a genuine form of who you are. I was always questioning myself. My identity was always fluid, never grounded.

I was born at a traumatic point in my family's history, directly after a significant death. I entered an environment of collective emotional numbness. Grief, like rejection, has many layers. It has little consideration for health, and can easily override love and reason.

Later, during my season of therapy, I discovered rejection found me in-utero, due to this family loss. This rejection was a result of the emotional ill-health of others, not who God made me to be. He had knit me together for greater purpose. But I didn't see or understand that until much later in life.

Due to this family turmoil, I was never going to be the 'golden child'. That role jumped around in my family but never landed on me. That doesn't mean I didn't aspire to that favoured spot, or unconsciously attempt to work towards earning it. Roles in narcissistic family structures are generally well-defined.

I don't remember the exact time I started struggling physically but, around my second year at primary school, I would run out of breath and experience pain when I overexerted myself. I was terrified of sport, so I avoided it. I wonder if that was why I retreated to books. It was a practical transition, but also satisfied my God-given vibrant imagination.

My aversion to sport was explained in 2020, when I was in hospital with the perforation. Coincidentally, I was also diagnosed with a pericardial effusion, a condition where fluid collects around the heart resulting in shortness of breath and pain in the chest. A pericardial effusion generally constitutes a life-threatening medical emergency, yet my 2020 body miraculously lived with it. I was treated with heavy medication to return the fluid to a normal level. It didn't move, and I now live with the fluctuating fluid. It doesn't drastically affect me now, but it would have when it started and explains my childhood lack of breath, pain, and resultant dread of sport.

'Why didn't you complain? It would have been horribly painful, so how did your parents not see you were struggling?' a specialist asked me, questions which revealed my childhood.

I don't remember complaining much as a child. Somewhere in my tiny mind, I had convinced myself that my existence didn't matter, that my pain and suffering wasn't important. I have very few recollections of my pain being voiced, heard, seen, or addressed. This was symptomatic of the place I believed I held in the family structure, the place of not mattering. I was the lost child, not the golden child. But the Lord, in His great mercy and love, gifted me a miracle I didn't even know I needed. Despite having a condition that could have killed me, I didn't die because the Lord gifted to my body the ability to withstand.

At the end of primary school, I was diagnosed with scoliosis and had to wear a brace for the next three years. I can still recall my hope that this would make me special and 'seen'. But it didn't. I remained uninteresting, and my inability to exert myself or even move effectively meant I put on a lot of weight. I remained the 'fat girl' throughout childhood, and only lost weight in my late teens, when exercise became easier (my body adapted to the heart condition), and I overcame my desire to soothe my emotional distress by eating—the one thing I could control. I had several self-soothing false refuges like food — now healed.

I worked hard to earn favour. I got into acting and theatre, had some academic success, and did my best to be affirmed with these endeavours—with limited impact. In my late teenage and young adult years, I tried to hide anything I did that I knew was unfavourable. In the meantime, I had no idea who I was, and I was a hot mess. My saving grace was that I left home. But that compounded my constant struggle to be relevant.

I remember the day I was told I had negatively impacted the family far more than the tragic death of my sister. It was a cruel blow. I was devastated, but I continued to participate in the game I didn't even realise I was playing.

Permanent change came when I married a man the family deemed unsuitable, a man who was never prepared to accept the way things were. The family begged us to invest in the family business, and we unwisely tried to earn favour by agreeing. It was a disaster. Irreversible damage was done, bondages established that lasted for seventeen years (that we sought desperately to get out of) and we experienced a time of hardship.

But one major thing changed in me. I stopped believing that God was who I had been told He was, and I sought a relationship with Jesus for myself. And over the years, things became clear to me regarding my family structure.

- ♪ Silence and displeasure are weapons of manipulation, intimidation, and punishment.
- ♪ It was unacceptable to expect an apology.
- ♪ Wrongdoing was rarely addressed or spoken about.
- ♪ Triangulation was the norm. Someone was always on the 'outer'.
- ♪ Words were enough. Actions didn't need to back up the words. It was unacceptable to think actions and words should match.
- ♪ History could be rewritten, always against me, or other family members who were suffering displeasure or punishment.
- ♪ 'Not recalling' is a viable excuse or exoneration.
- ♪ I should never expect to be in the right.
- ♪ My achievements would not be celebrated.
- ♪ I had to earn favour, but I would never be favoured.
- ♪ The achievements of other family members would be used as a weapon against my character or as an unfavourable comparison.
- ♪ I couldn't trust a gift. It could be used as a 'dig' at me, or given in lieu of righting a wrong, or in replacement of repentance.

- ♪ Truth was fluid, depending on narcissistic perspective. It was not safe to tell or share the truth.

- ♪ I was required to believe and support the version of events that suited the family rhetoric.

- ♪ My resources were to be used where deemed necessary, without return.

- ♪ I could never be confident in where I stood, and fight/flight/freeze was my normal state of being.

By the time my husband was diagnosed with cancer, I had recognised these symptoms, but I still didn't have a name for the problem or know how to overcome it.

My rebellion against my dysfunctional upbringing—my unwillingness to play the game, toe the line, live out my role, or be silent finally led me to be deemed permanently unacceptable. I was entrenched as the family scapegoat—a role I had, in truth, played for most of my adult life. However, I didn't realise this was my role until another encounter with narcissistic abuse, a year after my husband passed, sent me reeling and wondering. How did I fall into this trap? It was so familiar and read like a playbook of emotional upheaval and confusion.

At that time, I could have laid down and died. I felt abandoned, in horrible grief, desperately sick, struggling as a single mum and widow, worthless, cheated, abused, deeply distraught, humiliated, and lost.

But, because I sought the Lord for His understanding, He turned and healed me, reprogramed my thinking, and restored to me the identity He had always planned for me. He led me on a study of narcissistic abuse. I'd never heard of it before, but the symptoms were clear, concise, and applied to me.

I do not believe I was given this understanding so I could blame others or get stuck in a victim mentality. Nobody is good. We have all sinned and fallen short. That 'all' included me. I was a cog in that system. I made mistakes and contributed to it, even if I did eventually rebel and opt out. God had already done enormous work in me, revealing and healing all those layers of rejection that had come before, but I wasn't perfect or innocent, just seeking a full healing. This was the last layer, the foundation of my life that needed to be replaced, and I give humble thanks for everyone He placed in my life that led to that healing—even the people who hurt me.

Jesus began His healing work by inviting me to sit with Him on Easter Friday in 2021 as the ultimate Scapegoat, one for all time. He is the abandoned One who has never and will not abandon me. He removed that cornerstone of rejection in my life and replaced it with Himself, the rejected Cornerstone who saved and rescued me. He is all I need.

In the years since, He has gently brought me out of fight mode and into peace mode. He has rebuilt my identity from the foundation up. So many revelations and new things have come to pass. He has even given me both an adopted and a new family, and so many people who love and care for me and my son.

Rejection has no place with me. I forgive freely and wholly because I am free and wholly forgiven. When it comes to relationships, I walk in wisdom, guarding my heart, and knowing that relationship and forgiveness are not the same thing. Forgiveness is vital, required, compulsory. A restoration of relationship requires more than forgiveness. It requires repentance, and the building back of trust. It requires you to be an observer of the fruit.

> *'By their fruit you will recognise them. Do people pick grapes from thornbushes, or figs from thistles? Likewise, every good tree bears good fruit, but a bad tree bears bad fruit.'*
>
> *Matthew 7:16–17* NIV

Narcissistic abuse and rejection, though part of my story, are no longer a factor in my identity. And on this new foundation of Himself, the Lord continues to reveal who He made me to be. I continue to submit to Him, and seek His forgiveness, grace, and peace.

I am a work-in-progress, but I now KNOW who I am.

> *'It is for freedom that Christ has set us free. Stand firm, then, and do not let yourselves be burdened again by a yoke of slavery.'*
>
> *Galatians 5:1* NIV

# The Past is a Foreign Country

## MIRANDA DE JAGER

*The past is a foreign country; they do things differently there.*

*L.P. Hartley*

'Ladies and gentlemen, while the cabin crew prepares the plane for landing, please stash your tray tables; put your seats in the upright position and make sure your seatbelts are securely fastened.'

I check my seatbelt, place my handbag under the seat and hand my empty cup to a cabin crew member. When the lights are dimmed, I peek out the window to see the sun rising over Johannesburg, the contrast between tall buildings in affluent areas and the flat darkness of shanty towns. My normal enthusiasm over this magnificent view evades me today. I lean my head against the headrest and inhale in an attempt to relax, but uncertainty worms through my mind. Exhausted after a lengthy flight from Brisbane, sleep having evaded me for most of the flight; my mind plays out all the possible scenarios. What will I find when I get there? Am I ready to face her? I push the fear aside and remind myself that this challenging venture will be rewarding for both of us. I cannot leave her to her own devices any longer. She has been through so much that I cannot imagine how she managed to deal with it at her age.

Shepherding my thoughts back to the present, I gather my hand luggage, exit the plane and follow the crowded winding passage to clear customs. After I collect my checked bag, I make my way through the busy Johannesburg International airport, dodging the over-zealous self-appointed guides who offer to show me where to go. I know my way. Many travellers have been hoodwinked by trusting the wrong guide. With a take-away coffee, I make my way to car rentals.

The GPS guides my exit from the airport and onto the correct freeway.

After an hour's drive, I leave the freeway and follow a quiet country road. With fresh eyes after forty-five years, I gaze at the familiar scenery, noting that the grassy fields and gum trees could easily be mistaken for an Australian landscape. Fifteen minutes later, I see the entrance to the powerstation village. An engraving on the brick wall on either side of the road announces *Wilge Kragstasie*, 'Willow Power Station'. It's exactly as I remember it. I turn off the GPS. I lived here for the first eight years of my life.

I slow down so I can take in every detail: red brick houses on both sides of the road, all built in the same 50s style with quaint gardens and wire fencing, soccer field to the right with beautiful manicured lawns and a few swings for kids on the other side of the field. At the T-junction I turn right. There's the entrance to the large adult pool and the little gate to the square baby pool where my younger sister and I often swam. Further down the road is my childhood house on the corner block to the left, the familiar number '67' on the post-box mounded on a square wooden fence post. The round bus shelter across the road is still there. It was built from the same red bricks as the houses and has a thatch roof, openings for windows and a door at the far side. My sister and I caught the school bus at the next stop further down the road, but I clearly remember every detail of the benches all round the interior and the concrete floor. As fear enters my mind, I thrust the old memories aside and remind myself why I am here.

I park the car under a large tree and make my way through the small gate to the garden path leading to the front door. Mom used chalk to draw numbered hop-scotch shapes on the concrete path. Old memories flood my mind: the beautiful flowers she planted in nature beds around the front garden, the colourful butterflies I tried to catch for hours on end. The flowers are gone, but the lawn is in good shape and the coral tree in the centre is still there. It's not a huge tree, but my younger sister and I climbed it anyway. We broke the seed pods open and played with the seeds.

There's the smooth concrete veranda under a wooden pergola, painted in the same red as the roof. I remember how

Mom, Dad, my sister and I sat on this veranda many a night sipping cordial while Dad showed us the stars or Mom told us stories about her childhood. I make my way to the wood-panelled front door and knock.

A little girl with long, soft blonde hair and blue-green eyes opens the door. 'Hello Miranda, I was waiting for you.' She seems hesitant.

I crouch down so that I can look her in the eye. 'Hello Nanna.' Nanna is the nickname she gave herself when she started talking and couldn't pronounce her real name—I still fondly call her by this name. 'Your hair looks beautiful; did you wash it?'

She nods wordlessly and I stand up and hold out my hand. 'Would you like to show me the house?' She takes my hand uncertainly and I am surprised that her emotions are so well-controlled. When I look into her eyes, I see wisdom beyond her age. She is only six years old but so composed.

We walk into the entrance hall and pause at the first door on the left. 'This is the sitting room.' She points to the fireplace. 'That's where Daddy makes a fire in the winter and where he sits in the chair near it with his pipe and a book.' We continue to the square kitchen. 'This is where we eat.' It has traditional wooden cabinetry and an old enamel white stove on four curved legs. Underneath the stove is a saucer of milk for the cats. There is an oval melamine table with four chairs in the centre and a huge old fridge against the wall opposite the back door. There is a screen door as well as an outside door with a window at the top. The back garden is small but functional with a well-kept lawn and a long clothesline. I glance up at the row of traditional cake tins displayed on a top cabinet above the melamine worktop.

Nanna follows my glance and says, 'There is a wasp nest behind that tin. If we don't want to eat our vegetables, Mom calls the wasp to come and sting us.'

I smile. 'Do you really think the wasp will do that?'

Her little face is serious. 'Oh yes, one day while Mom was calling him, the door was open and he came flying in. He didn't sting us because we quickly ate our veggies. He just circled the table and went into his mud nest.'

We make our way down the passage and she shows me the guest room, bathroom and main bedroom. As we reach the room at the end of the passage, she stops. 'My younger sister and I share this room.'

Two single beds with a bedside cabinet in the middle with a lamp on a crocheted doily. There is a built-in closet next to the window. Looking out, I see the huge peach tree and recall a tea party under the branches, drinking real tea from my tiny tea set and eating cake. A flood of old memories surface but I push them aside. I am here for Nanna, not for myself.

She sits down on her bed. 'This is my bed.' There's a suitcase next to it.

I sit beside her and look her in the eye. 'Nanna, do you know why I'm here?'

She nods.

'Are you still willing to come home with me?'

She nods, but there are tears in her eyes. 'I wish I could talk to someone, but nobody understands me.'

I squeeze her hand gently. 'You can talk to me. You can tell me anything and I promise I will do my best to understand.'

She smiles for the first time. 'My bag is already packed. Can I bring my toys too?'

I smile. 'Of course you can. Come on, let's go.' I take the suitcase and she grabs a bag of toys. I push the sadness of old memories away.

Holding her hand, we exit onto the veranda. I close the front door with a finality that surprises me. I load up the luggage in the car and drive to a local holiday resort where we swim and have fun together for a few days.

After a long flight home, Nanna stares as we enter my house in Brisbane. I carry the bags inside and show Nanna her new bedroom. She loves the pink curtains and floral doona. I show her our large open-plan living area, then push back the sliding doors to the patio. Two little fluffy white dogs come running inside, tails wagging. Lucy, the toy poodle, sneezes in excitement and Simba, a miniature Maltese, gives a cheeky bark. They greet me, sniff Nanna and lick her toes. She giggles, drops down to the floor and hugs them. She screams with laughter as they lick her face.

While Nanna plays with the dogs, I pour cordial and arrange cookies in a plate. As we eat in the living room, the dogs jump onto the couch as I look at Nanna. 'My husband is still at work, but I will introduce you to him tonight.' My mind goes back to all this little girl has had to endure. I swallow my tears. 'He is a good man. You do not need to be afraid of him, because he will never hurt you. Do you understand what I mean?'

Nanna nods but there is fear in her eyes.

I continue, 'He loves kids and he is excited to meet you. You have your own bedroom now and you are welcome to lock the door whenever you want to. We can practice it to make sure you know how the lock works.'

'Mom never allowed us to lock our bedroom door, we always had to leave it open a crack.'

'I know, and that is why I said that in this house you are allowed to lock your door if you want to. I want you to know that you are safe now.'

She nods while tears flow. I hold her tightly and whisper, 'I wish I could take away all your heartache and pain. I will pray with you that Jesus will heal you and take away the deep hurt that feels like it's stuck in your tummy.'

She pulls away, surprised. 'How do you know about the hurt in my tummy?'

'My dearest Nanna, don't you know who I am? I am you. You are a broken part of me that remained locked away in my past. I left you in my childhood home, because the knowledge of what happened to us there and in the bus shelter was too great to bear. I appreciate the intelligent way in which you withheld the anguish, while allowing me to remember only the happy parts of our childhood. Your bravery secured my survival and assisted me to build healthy relationships and a successful career. I owe you so much, because you offered yourself to save me. Your sadness was buried so deep that I was hardly aware of it. I know that you were patiently waiting for the right time and hoping that I will discover you. By the grace of God, my memory has returned and I know about the horrific circumstances you had to face. That is why I decided that it was time to take a virtual journey to my childhood home to bring you back. I want you to be part of my life.'

As her tears continue to flow, I wipe away my own. I ask God to heal her pain and make her whole so she can grow up to be my age. That one day we will be reunited into a whole human being.

My journey down memory lane was worthwhile and I know God will complete the amazing work that He started in my life when my repressed memories started to surface. We have a good life in Australia; this is the perfect environment to continue my recovery process.

# As in the Natural

## ANNE HAMILTON

*D*on't think—just do it.

I'd just seen an ad for an extraordinary deal—a less-than-half-price return airfare to the Cook Islands. I'm not impulsive but cautious, so I knew if I didn't act immediately, I'd come up with half a dozen reasons why heading off to a tropical paradise was a *really* bad idea. So I didn't think. I didn't pray. I just looked at the available dates and bought a ticket for eight months in the future.

And then, having committed myself to the unimaginably crazy, I sat back and asked myself why on earth I'd done it. And what came to mind was all the times when my dad was stressed or overwhelmed with trouble that he'd said, 'I just want to lie on a beach in the Cook Islands for a week.'

Yet he never went.

But it was a constant refrain. And it was a peculiar saying because my dad loathed travel. He detested even thinking about it.

So there it was. I was going to the Cook Islands because my dad never did and clearly it was something so deeply laid on his heart that, despite his reluctance to go anywhere much further than an hour or so from home, he couldn't stop expressing the desire to go.

For the first time, I wondered why. *So*, I said to God, *what's the real reason for going to the Cook Islands? What assignment was my dad supposed to complete?*

~~Cut the spiritual supply lines~~

*Right*, says me to meself, having only the vaguest idea what that meant, *who should I take with me?* The way I figured it was, if I was imagining God speaking to me, the worst that could happen was a week's holiday on a sun-kissed island in the middle of the Pacific Ocean. And if I wasn't imagining it, then this would be a significant task within the heavenly realm.

~~Ask Janice and Janette~~

I did. They managed to score the same deal and booked tickets too.

*Supply lines*, I pondered over the next few months. *An army cannot advance beyond its supply line or it will have to retreat and lose the ground it has gained.* During the First World War in the Middle East, it was the Pacific Islanders who solved the problem of supplying the troops advancing up the desert road from Egypt into the Holy Land. Trucks were noisy, making them an easy target for enemy attack, and they were apt to get stuck in the sand as well as lost in the trackless dunes.

The Islanders offered a simple way to overcome all these problems: a craft that almost no-one had heard of until that time—a catamaran. No engine to give its position away, no precious petrol needed to power it, no difficulty in loading it up with stores, no need for a harbour to bring it in to shore, no need for a road. As for finding the way—easy as. Its navigators would steer by the stars. *Tell us where you want it delivered,* the Islanders said, *and we'll get it there.*

*As in the natural, so in the spiritual,* I thought. *That's the blessings the people of the Pacific have for the world. They are the navigators who keep the spiritual supply lines open.* Then it dawned on me. *If God has tasked me with cutting the supply lines, they must be polluted.* Then another thought intruded. *Spiritual supply lines would have to connect sacred sites. And these feel like they are scattered across the globe. I think they're on mountains. A* significant obstacle occurred to me. *I don't have the authority to do this. I don't think Janice or Janette do either.*

Obstacles are really just opportunities for God to show Himself strong on our behalf.

I was in New Zealand for a conference not long after these disturbing thoughts surfaced when a man came up to me and said, 'The Lord has told me you have a message for me.'

I shook my head. 'I don't do personal prophecy. But… okay… maybe I have a message I don't know about. What's your name?'

He told me. It meant nothing.

'Where do you come from?'

Still nothing. I looked him over, wondering if he had Māori heritage. 'What's your iwi?' I asked.

'You mean tribe?' he said.

*I used the right word*, I thought. *Why didn't he?*

As soon as he revealed his affiliations, I knew I did indeed have a message for him. But, at that moment, I was called to the stage. 'Catch you at morning tea,' I said to him as I hurried off.

I was about to step onto the platform when someone grabbed my sleeve. 'Whatever you do,' the person whispered, 'don't give the message in private. Make sure it's in public.'

*Oh goodness*, I wondered, *what have I stepped into?* But then I had an inspiration. I could weave the message I needed to deliver into my talk. So I simply added some thoughts about mountains—because, for Māori people, identity is bound up with, first, the sacred mountain, second, the sacred river, third, their iwi.

'You know what?' I asked the audience. 'Here, in this country, when you are asking God to help your family, you need to be like Caleb when he went and said, "Give me this mountain."'

I had barely got a foot off the stage when the man I'd asked to meet me at morning tea was right in front of my face. 'What mountain?'

'You know exactly what mountain,' I told him.

'What's its name?'

'You know its name.'

We tussled for several minutes until I gave in and told him the name.

'I knew you were going to say that,' he sighed. 'I can't do it. You don't understand. I'm too afraid.'

Actually, given the high level of spiritual darkness on that particular peak, I did have some small glimpse of the giants he needed to face.

He paused. 'I'll give you my mantle, and you can do it.'

'No. It's your assignment.'

'It's a royal mantle,' he said. 'Please.'

Now I paused. 'Let me ask the Holy Spirit.' I prayed silently. 'Can I have a loan of your mantle?' I said after half a minute. 'There's something I have to do later this year that I don't have the authority for, but involves praying about your mountain and another mountain in the middle of the Pacific.'

He nodded and promised to keep in touch. But when I emailed him there was no reply.

Nothing daunted, Janice, Janette and I set off for a week on Rarotonga in the Cook Islands in September that year. It took most of our time there to realise that we had a perfect view of the mountain we were looking for straight out the front window of the house we'd rented.

Did we have any idea what we were doing? No. Not at all. We just asked for the ungodly supply lines to be cut between the mountain in Rarotonga that shared a name with one in New Zealand.

We prayed as best we could, our words inadequate and trivial. *It's not about us and the power of our words,* we reminded ourselves, *it's about Jesus as our mediator.* Each of us privately thought to ourselves that we'd never know the outcome of our prayer in this lifetime, whatever way it went.

The following afternoon after our prayer, we boarded a flight back to Sydney. We'd had an exotic holiday but felt a little deflated. The plane sat on the tarmac for nearly two hours. It transpired that there was not enough fuel to get the aircraft to Sydney and the pilots had been negotiating with Tonga to refuel there.

Around midnight, the plane descended to Tonga. But the authorities there also had a supply problem. They weren't willing to give over sufficient fuel to get to Sydney, just to Auckland. I was sitting there, looking out the window at the dazzling lights in the darkened airport terminal and I said to God, *Is this retaliation for praying what we did about the mountain?*

~~WHAT DID YOU ASK FOR?~~

*For the supply lines to be cut.* In that moment, with a frisson of wonder, I realised that we were experiencing exactly that. *A cutting of fuel supply.*

~~AS IN THE NATURAL, SO IN THE SPIRITUAL~~

At that moment, Janice caught my eye. We looked at each other and realised we'd both been thinking the same thing about backlash. And when we checked with each other, we found we'd both got the same answer.

~~AS IN THE NATURAL, SO IN THE SPIRITUAL~~

I have to admit that, although I eventually thanked God, that wasn't my first reaction. *You know,* I said to Him, *I've got so used to waiting twenty years for an answer to prayer that I never expect You to respond immediately.*

*So, please, next time You decide to answer straight away, could You just warn me in advance so I can plan a quick getaway?*

# The Tea Set

## DELL SADDLER HAMILTON

*'He set it apart to the Lord.'*

*Numbers 7:1* NIRV

My Mum, Mary, had a very special tea set, far too good for everyday use. The finest of bone china, exquisitely hand-painted, it consisted of eight dainty cups and saucers. It was a set fit for a visit by the queen. I inherited it and locked it in my display cabinet. Eventually I passed the set on to my second daughter. However, like me, she's never found an occasion worthy enough to bring it out to the table. In fact, in the hundred years since my father gave it to my mother, it's only been used once.

That was in 1938, twenty years after the end of the Great War—the 'war to end all wars'. The Depression had climaxed, yet our farm eleven kilometres outside of Nambour was still regularly visited by men looking for work. They were always given a feed, but only a few were ever given employment.

This particular day, a scruffy swaggie with a wooden leg limped his way up the hill to our farm. His name, I was told, was Tommy Atkins. For many years, I doubted that—after all, 'Tommy Atkins' was slang for a common soldier in the British Army as early as the nineteenth century. However, it really was his name.

When he arrived, he was greeted warmly by both my parents. I was just eight years old and I remember my mum setting the table with a beautiful cloth and bringing out the never-previously-or-subsequently-used tea set. We sat down to hot buttered scones and sipped tea from tiny cups of delicate bone china.

Thomas Atkins is the reason my family exists. Like my dad, Ernest Sadler—yes, only one 'd' in those days!—Tommy had enlisted early during the First World War. Dad had only been in Australia for three or four years when he became the 408th man from Queensland to join up, expecting to fight on the Western Front in France.

Dad was attached to 26 Infantry Battalion out of Brisbane while Tommy belonged to 20 Infantry Battalion from Sydney. After setting sail, both Tommy and Dad found their Anzac units detoured to Gallipoli. Somewhere in Egypt or the Dardanelles, they met up and became best mates.

So, when Dad failed to return from a mission just three weeks after arriving at Gallipoli, Tommy scrambled out to find him. Dad was unconscious, near death and bleeding profusely from a head wound. Part of his skull had been sheared off and bits of bone and shrapnel were embedded in his brain.

Tommy picked him up, took him to a First Aid station and threatened the medics with courtmartial when they said they needed to devote their attention to those who had even a slim chance of survival, not none. A few days later, still in a coma, Dad was taken to a hospital ship bound for Britain. It stopped in at Gibraltar and there, waiting for transport to take them to England, were the four top neurosurgeons in the world at the time. With little better to do, they occupied themselves with picking the slivers of shrapnel and bone from my dad's brain.

And, of course, he eventually recovered—or I wouldn't be able to tell the tale. But he had significant memory loss. He never remembered having fought at Gallipoli and thought his wounds were sustained in France—that, after all, was the place where all the original Anzac battalions thought they were heading before being rerouted to the Dardanelles.

After the withdrawal from Gallipoli, the remnants of Tommy's battalion headed off to the trenches of France. It was there he lost his leg.

My mum rightly treated Tommy as royalty when he came to visit that day in 1938, on the eve of another global conflict. It took me a long time to realise the holiness and sacredness attached to drinking tea and eating hot scones with a swagman. Yet these treasured cups and plates had always been 'set apart'—and 'set apart' is indeed what holiness and consecration means.

The respect my parents showed that day has stayed with me all my life as a model of what holiness means: we honour you.

# Rowena's Boy

## ROSEMARY NEW

*It* *must have been devastating for Dad, when his sister died* *suddenly a thousand miles away.* I held onto the only picture of Rowena I could find amongst all Dad's photographs in his velvet-lined wooden box. Hand-written in faded ink on the back was *Rowena, Debutante 1931.* The black and white studio photo was composed very formally, showing head and shoulders only. *That was in the Depression,* I realised. *Rowena's white gown would have been very simply styled.*

I gazed out the window, deep in thought. My dad and Rowena were only one year apart in age, and he had only ever spoken about her fondly, but with great sadness. *He probably was her debutante partner,* I thought. Although I would never know, it made sense. He would have proudly escorted Rowena for her 'coming out.'

Holding the photo very carefully, I inserted it into a blank envelope on the table. I had to bring it today. The last two weeks had been a whirlwind since the phone call that changed everything. It had been raining all day, making it peacefully quiet, when the phone rang late in the afternoon.

'Rosemary?'

'Yes…'

'Hi… I'm Brock… I think we are cousins.'

I didn't respond for a moment. 'What? Brock? Who?'

'Is your father's name Ronald?'

'Yes…'

'Did he have a sister named Rowena?'

'Yes.' My quiet afternoon began to feel disquieting. 'But she died.'

'Well… she was my mother. I'm Brock Ralston.'

Breathless, I reached as far as the telephone cord allowed to grab a chair. 'But… where are you? Where've you been? How did you find me?'

Brock's questions starting pouring out. 'Is your father still alive?'

'Yes. He's 87 now but he's got dementia. He's in a nursing home.' I thought I heard sobs at the other end of the phone.

'He's still alive? He's my Uncle Ron! You're my mother's only relatives…'

We chatted through tears and missing years. Brock knew very little; I didn't think I knew much more.

'All I know,' Brock said presently, 'is that I was only nine months old—and Dad wouldn't ever talk about it.'

'Oh.' *Should I say what I know?* My heart was racing. *How could he not know? Should I tell Brock?* No...

'My dad loved your mother—she was his little sister—he often said how close they were.' I had to think fast. *Dad had burdened me with her story...* 'But when she died, my parents had already moved here to Queensland. They lost everything in the 1949 cyclone. Your mum died the next year—they had no money to go back for Rowena's funeral.'

*I was talking too fast...* 'It broke my dad's heart, I think, that he couldn't even say good-bye. Dad always said your father didn't keep in touch afterwards, so no one ever knew what happened to you. Dad assumed he remarried, because you were just a baby.'

'Yes,' Brock said, 'Dad did re-marry. My step-mother was as good as any mother could be, but I never found out about my real mother's family. I've been looking for years, but all Ronald's brothers have passed on.'

'Yes, they have. And their older sister Clara died two years ago.'

'My mother had a *SISTER!*'

'Yes, she was beautiful. I loved Aunty Clara. I've got photos of her I'll send to you! I didn't really know my uncles. I don't think they ever came up here to visit.'

'Can I come and see my Uncle Ron?' Brock sounded desperate. 'I want to meet my mother's brother. I live in North Queensland, but I can come the week after next.'

My heart lifted. 'Oh, yes please!'

The next two weeks released something precious that had long been lost. Every day I sat searching through the jumble of old photos in Dad's wooden box, digging around for any clues to fill in gaps for Brock. I'd never been interested in this muddled pile of sombre-looking men with moustaches and stern women with frilly lace high around their necks. But I did find a yellowed piece of paper on which was scribbled Dad's family tree! They were all now deceased, except Dad: his four brothers, Clara, and Rowena. So I neatly printed beneath Rowena's name: 'Brock.'

Thankfully some of the photographs had ink descriptions written on the back. *Dad never got around to putting these into an album, and I don't know who any of these people are.* I had a shoebox of printed photos just as disorganised. *I must do something with all my photographs... soon!* But mine would have to wait.

This morning I was waiting for Brock to arrive, so I could drive us both to Dad's nursing home. Brock was coming from way up north—I hoped he hadn't driven through the night. I couldn't imagine how it would feel to meet a relative for the very first time, but felt excited that Brock would at last see his uncle. I hoped beyond hope that Dad's mind would be clear this morning—so that the visit would be healing for my cousin.

I was ready early, and I admit to feeling just a little nervy when I heard his car stopping out front of my house. Although he was a stranger, we were family—lost for all my life, as Rowena died before I was born. I walked out to greet Brock—he looked a bit like Dad, but much younger.

'Brock!' I offered to hug. It was odd, yet familiar. 'Do you want to freshen up before we go there?'

'No, I'm ready, I stayed in that motel 100k back up the road last night. Thought I'd get a good sleep, but I had too many thoughts running through my head. I got away just before daylight.'

'That's exactly what Dad always says!' Familiarity was right there! 'Good! Let's set off, because he won't even know who I am if we don't get there early.'

Brock and I sat together quietly in my car as I handed him the envelope. 'I found this photo of your mother… it's the only one I could find.'

He slowly pulled it out, and stared at Rowena's beautiful young face for the longest minute before he spoke. 'Where was this?'

'She was a debutante. It's written on the back. I think my dad would have been her partner but I don't know.' *I don't know what else to say… this might be an awkward silence all the way to the nursing home…* I started the engine for our 25-kilometre drive.

Brock tentatively repeated the question I didn't want to answer. 'I don't know what happened… I mean, how my mother died. Dad wouldn't ever talk about it. All I know…' His words became slower. '… is that I was only nine months old…'

I drew breath, and quietly prayed for wisdom. The scene unfolding in my mind's eye was terrible, how could I tell Rowena's son what happened when he sat on his mother's lap? 'Dad told me,' I began carefully. 'Your father was driving his new car. He had just bought it.'

'Come on, Row! I'll take us out for a ride! It's like floating on air, this one, and it goes really fast! Where would you like to go? We can go right down to the Quay and come back up that steep hill—really test it out!'

'Oh, I don't know. What about the baby?'

'He'll be fine. You just sit him on your lap. The wind will blow on that cute little blonde curl of his. You'll love it!'

Rowena stood, hesitating. She should be putting Brock down soon for his sleep. But the new car looked so smart, and smelled so leathery, and… was it really, truly fast?

'We can get down to the Quay and back again before the sun goes down. I want you both to be the first ones to ride in our new car!'

Rowena disappeared inside the house to collect a couple of warm wraps for the baby. If indeed the car did go fast, she would need to wrap Brock snugly against the late afternoon chill through her window. She lifted Brock out from his cot where he had been propped up with some cuddly toys. With the baby blankets over one arm and Brock on the other, she came out to the car.

Rick proudly opened the passenger door for them. He looked like a concierge, motioning with a broad sweep of his arm, for the Lady of the House and his little Prince Charming. Rowena sat down on the cushiony, black leather seat. She wrapped Brock neatly into the blue bunny rug and sat him down against her stomach, holding him with her left arm and placing the extra wrap on the bench seat between herself and Rick.

He smiled at her, and gave Brock a tickle under his chubby chin. Then with both feet on the pedals and one hand holding the steering wheel, he turned on the ignition. The engine sweetly purred. Rowena smiled at him. He looked so happy, so pleased with himself. And so he should be! He had worked hard to afford this fancy new car!

*Rick gently changed up through the gears to the top speed of 60 miles-per-hour, speeding along the narrow bitumen road towards the Quay. The rushing wind blew into Rowena's passenger window, fluffing Brock's blonde baby curls. She didn't speak, just enjoyed sitting there feeling special.*

*At the Quay, Rick stopped so they could admire the yachts bobbing around in the harbour. It was peaceful looking at the water, glinting in the late afternoon sun, yacht sails fluttering in the breeze. Brock started fidgeting. 'We'd better head home, Rick, he's getting tired and he hasn't had his tea yet.'*

*Rick started the car and turned out of the Quay-side exit. 'We'll go back up this steep hill—test out the engine.' Dropping back through the gears, he powered the car though the left-hand turn and accelerated up the hill.*

*The whole world stopped. Glass and blood, and Brock was screaming. Rick's car was crushed on the passenger side. Rick couldn't see Rowena, only a great big tray where she had been sitting. Urgently, he scrambled underneath it to reach and grab the baby, then pushed their way out of the wreck.*

I dared not look at Brock as I struggled to find the right words. 'There was a truck broken down up the hill road. Your dad never saw it because the afternoon sun was blinding his eyes. He drove straight into the tray of the truck.' *I can't ever tell him the rest,* I decided.

Brock nodded respectfully. 'My poor Dad…' Then he held his mother's photo against his heart a long, long time, before slipping it into his shirt pocket.

At the nursing home, Brock walked beside me through front reception into the residents' morning area. My father was lounging listlessly in a recliner beside a garden window. I walked over and touched him gently on his arm. 'Dad?'

He looked up. *He recognised me!* The light was in his eyes this morning. Smiling, he hauled his emaciated body from the chair to wrap me within his thin, white arms. 'Rosemary!'

I grasped Dad's elbows, and looked into his happy face. 'Dad! I've brought you a visitor—Brock Ralston.'

Brock put his hand forward. 'Uncle Ron!'

Dad clung to the hand-shake like he never wanted to let go. In ecstatic realisation he exclaimed, 'ROWENA'S BOY! I *knew* you would turn out alright!'

He staggered, swaying. Brock held onto his Uncle Ron as I helped guide them back to Dad's recliner, lowering his weak body into the chair. Dad looked at us blankly. The light in his eyes was gone.

Brock searched my face. 'How long has he got?'

*It probably won't be long now.* 'He's longed after you all your life. His soul has found peace now.' *There's nothing left to hold him here anymore.* 'He's a man of faith, you know.'

'I'll come back when he goes,' Brock told me. He stepped away from his Uncle Ron, who was drifting off to sleep.

Neither of us spoke as we quietly left. No words could have described the healing that just took place. I glanced at my cousin. *There's light in your eyes now, Brock!*

*Ronald 1909–1997*
*Rowena 1910–1950*

# Shining Face of God

## ANTONI BONETTI AM

With various orchestras that I have conducted over fifty years, prayer is as vital for an uplifting performance as is prior practice and rehearsals. My school orchestras have had a roster so that students can volunteer to offer a short prayer before rehearsals. Before conducting performances, I sit quietly in the green room for a few minutes' silent prayer.

Directing adult community orchestras, I have often prayed with other musicians that God would bless these performances; that He would speak to those in the audience and be present with orchestra members. Often, people have come up after those performances and said that they were listening to more than music. In one particular situation after praying together, God made us very much aware of His presence.

Brisbane Symphony Orchestra performed Joseph Haydn's oratorio *The Creation* in a poorly lit Brisbane church in Ann Street. The weather was gloomy and overcast.

In the *Creation* oratorio, three soloists represent the archangels Raphael, Uriel and Gabriel, as well as Adam and Eve. They, and a full choir, are accompanied by a Classical orchestra which for this work includes trombones and contra bassoon.

Some members of the choir and orchestra had expressed Christian faith so I invited them to join me beforehand in the crypt. Together, we prayed for God to be in our midst.

The work starts with a slow, quiet orchestral introduction, titled *The Representation of Chaos*. After 60 bars a small basso recitative (Raphael) commences:

> *In the beginning God made Heaven and earth; and the Earth was without form and void, and darkness was over the face of the waters.*

After a further orchestral interlude of 20 bars, the choir commences singing:

> *... and God said: Let there be Light, and there was Light* (bar 86)

—to which the full tutti orchestra plays fortissimo.

As the choir sang the second word *'Light'*, a sunbeam shone through the west window, blinding the 1st violin section.

The smiles on the faces that had earlier prayed with me shone with... *light!*

God was indeed there. We imagined His voice and chuckle: 'You want *light*...? I'll give you *light!*'

First performed in 1798, this *'light'* moment created a sensation when the work was first rehearsed in public. A friend of Haydn's wrote: 'At that moment when light broke out for the first time, one would have said that rays darted from the composer's burning eyes. The enchantment of the electrified Viennese was so general that the orchestra could not proceed for some minutes.'

An audience member wrote, 'Already three days have passed since that happy evening, and it still sounds in my ears and heart, and my breast is constricted by many emotions even thinking of it.'

A year before his death, Haydn attended a performance on 27 March, 1808. Frail, ill and nearly blind, Haydn was carried in on an armchair. It's said that the audience broke into spontaneous applause at the coming of *'light.'* Haydn weakly pointed upwards and said: 'Not from me—everything comes from up there!'

# AUTHORS

## HAZEL BARKER

Hazel was born in Burma of an Iranian Muslim father and an English Catholic mother. Blacklisted by the Burmese Junta, she fled to Australia, where her heart's desires were fulfilled when she married the boy of her dreams. Her short stories, memoirs and literary novels have won many awards. Three were finalists in the Australia and New Zealand CALEB Competitions of 2017, 2019 and 2022, respectively.

## LINDA BARTON

Linda Barton, like many women, wears many hats: daughter, wife, mother, and employee. Recently, with the support of family and friends, she co-founded a grassroots charity, *Hike to Heal Australia*, to proactively promote suicide prevention and mental health awareness in her local community. Linda's short stories are written to highlight God's grace, offering hope and inspiration to those in need.

## ANTONI BONETTI AM

Antoni Bonetti AM is the founding conductor of Brisbane Symphony Orchestra and Noosa Orchestra. He lectured at both the Conservatorium and UQ, completing a Master of Music. He has performed and conducted across Australia, USA, Europe and New Zealand.

London-born, Antoni played with the Australian Symphony Orchestras, freelanced with New Philharmonia Orchestra and London Mozart Players, and was concertmaster of

Norrlands Opera, Sweden and the Queensland Theatre Orchestra. He toured St Peters Lutheran College orchestra to Europe, New Zealand and nationally. He teaches at St Aidan's and Good Shepherd College, Noosaville.

## RUTH BONETTI

Stories of real people, past and present, fascinate Ruth Back Bonetti. Her career in classical music became a passport to the world. Destiny led her to Sweden and Finland where she researched her grandfather's story, and that of the black-sheep brother who in 1899 dodged conscription into the Russian army—pursued to Suez. Her award-winning *Midnight Sun to Southern Cross* trilogy (historical biography/memoir) includes *The Art Deco Mansion in St Lucia*. Ruth's music, education and performance publications include two with Oxford University Press. Ruth founded Omega Writers in 1991. She was the Principal Clarinet with QYO, 1966–1972.

## DIANA DAVISON

Diana Davison lives in Queensland, Australia. Her work has appeared in *Poetica Christi Press Poetry* anthologies, *Stories of Life* short stories, *Grieve* Hunter Writers Centre anthologies in Australia and a small scattering of publications overseas —Wicked Shadow Press, Haiku Spirit, Time Haiku, Failed Haiku, Daily Haiku Leaf, Presence, Enchanted Garden Haiku and Shadow Pond Journal. She remains inspired by nature, family and the constant changes life presents.

## ROSE DEE

Rose Dee has published five novels. Two from her *Resolution* series have won CALEB Awards. She has also released *The Greenfield Legacy*, a collaborative novel, and standalone novel, *Ehvah After*. Her novels are inspired by the love of her coastal home and desire to produce exciting and contemporary stories of faith for women. Some of the resources that the Lord used to secure her freedom from narcissistic abuse are:

- Every book by Anne Hamilton (particularly: *Dealing with Azazel: Spirit of Rejection*)
- VMTC Prayer Ministry
- Christian Counselling
- Lots of internet searches about narcissistic nature, abuse and family structures.

## MIRANDA DE JAGER

Miranda de Jager grew up in South Africa where childhood challenges cultivated her passion to overcome hardship and encourage others. She started working at eighteen, obtained a degree while working full time and pursued an IT career. Miranda and her husband moved to Brisbane in 2010 and became Australian Citizens four years later. Miranda is fond of reading and enjoys anything creative, including sewing, painting and writing poetry.

## M. LESTER DIGHTON

Bishop M. Lester Dighton was born and raised in Queensland in a Humanistic environment with strong occult influences. While conducting various occult studies himself, he had an encounter with God which completely changed his life. He is now a self-supported Evangelical Preacher, who works individually with small groups and people in need in a variety of ways, and is a Chaplain to those whom he can serve.

## MICHELLE DENNIS EVANS

With contagious zest for life, bestselling author Michelle Dennis Evans creates words and wellness. This vibrant Gold Coast creative pours her imagination into young adult novels and free verse poetry, while inspiring others on their health journeys. When not writing or mentoring, Michelle embraces life's adventures with her spunky husband and four grown children, living out her belief that everyone is created to create. Connect with Michelle at **michelledennisevans.com**

## SANDRA FLORENTINA

Sandra Florentina is a pseudonym for a registered psychologist. She has been a Christian for 42 years. Her passion is living for Christ. She has worked with many people of faith including leaders, pastors, and elders. This is the first story that she has written. She believes the Holy Spirit laid the words of the story on her heart therefore she gives all the glory to Him.

## TERRY GATFIELD

Born under the sound of Bow Bells when the Luftwaffe was decimating the London landscape. Came to Brisbane at the dawn of the hippie movement. Tamed by one wife and four wonderful children plus their delightful 10 offspring. Taught at various universities, collected a handful of degrees. Travelled Asia, learnt Chinese. Published and conferenced about 100 papers. Retired now in a blissful ecological environment to play the flute and write the occasional book.

## ANNE HAMILTON

Anne was a mathematics teacher for 30 years before she decided one day it possibly wasn't her calling. She then realised she'd better apply for some jobs just to practise her interview skills. The first position she tried for was at *Vision Christian Media* and she was appointed the Australian editor of the devotional, *The Word for Today*. She is a speaker, editor, counsellor and award-winning author of 45 books. Listen (or read) her podcast at **gracedropswithanne.com**.

## DELL SADDLER HAMILTON

1930–2022

Dell was an agent of grace and healing to many wounded people all around the world. She ministered in Australia, New Zealand and Asia and often hosted many people from interstate and overseas who came to seek out her wisdom. She always wanted to write a book on angels and miracles. Included in this collection are two of the short stories she wrote about her true-life experiences before she died.

## PAMELA JULIAN

As a non-fiction writer, Pamela finds the joy and struggles of life experience provide a rich resource for writing from a faith-based perspective. She has had a number of devotions, life stories and poems published in various anthologies. This year is a return to writing, and includes a potential venture into fiction. Pamela enjoys art and a good book.

## NOLA LORRAINE

Nola Lorraine loves weaving words of faith, courage and hope. Her inspirational historical novel *Scattered* was a finalist in the 2021 CALEB Awards; and she has more than 150 short publications, including fiction, poetry, devotions, true stories, magazine articles and academic papers. She and her husband Tim run a freelance writing and editing business, *The Write Flourish*. She'd love to connect with you through her website: **www.nolalorraine.com.au**

## ROSEMARY NEW

Rosemary New often wondered how to relate the extraordinary moment when her father and his sister's son met for the first time. *'I chose to write within this narrative setting, using the graphic heart-wrenching details that Dad had only once given me. I witnessed the healing of two hearts at once—Dad's overwhelming joy, and my new cousin's astonished gratitude. My own incredible experience of God's grace can now be shared.'*

## RAELENE PURTILL

Raelene Purtill has been an active member of the Brisbane writing community since 2012.  Her short stories have been published in local and Australia-wide anthologies. She loves to connect with other writers through workshops, retreats and seminars, and to encourage new writers on their journey. To this end she facilitates a local writing group in the northern suburbs of Brisbane. Her work in progress is a steam punk dragon fantasy with Christian themes.

## REBEKAH ROBINSON

Rebekah Robinson just wants everyone to fall in love with Jesus Christ. Freelancing via Beckon Creative as a graphic designer, she enjoys singing, songwriting and worship leading, and may have a slight digital scrapbooking addiction. Rebekah has written *Someone to Look Up To*, and with Anne Hamilton, the first three books in the ongoing *DNA of God* series — *Core Values: Love, Joy* and *Peace,* featuring several of her Biblical vignettes.

## KAREN ROPER

Karen Roper is passionate about seeing people live their lives the way God intended and to fulfil the purpose and plans that God has for them. She has run several life groups and taught teen church and Sunday school.  She loves ministering to others one on one. She has authored two non-fiction books and writes a weekly blog at **livingthelifegodintended.com**.

## JO WANMER

Jo Wanmer writes to tell of her God and the wonderful things He has done. Her first book was written to display God's work in her life. You will find it hidden in the fiction story, *Though the Bud be Bruised*. Recently published, her new book, *El Shaddai*, displays God as a lover of our souls. Her hope is that her reader sees God revealed in her words.

## JENNY WOOLSEY

Jenny Woolsey, M.Ed. (Hons), is an author, speaker, potter and carer. She was born with a facial difference and lives with low vision. Jenny is an Amazon best-seller and has published eight middle grade/YA books on being different and a personal development book. Her short stories are published in 23 anthologies. Jenny volunteers in the community and mentors at the Queensland Writers Centre.

## JUSTIN YEEND

Drawing inspiration from both Renaissance and contemporary mystical Christian writers, Justin began his journey into fiction writing during his recent theological studies. This short story marks his first exploration of reimagining Biblical characters through a modern, contemplative lens. Justin resides in Brisbane with his wife and two children.

www.ingramcontent.com/pod-product-compliance
Lightning Source LLC
Chambersburg PA
CBHW060547190726
48283CB00003B/909